ETERNAL
SUMMER

ETER NAL SUM MER

FRANZISKA GÄNSLER

*Translated from the
German by
Imogen Taylor*

OTHER PRESS
New York

Originally published in German as *Ewig Sommer* in 2022 by Kein & Aber AG,
Zürich – Berlin
Copyright © 2022 by Kein & Aber AG, Zürich – Berlin.
All rights reserved.
Translation copyright © 2025 by Other Press

The translation of this book was supported by a grant from
the Goethe-Institut.

Image on pages i, iii, and v by Vandathai / Shutterstock.com

Production editor: Yvonne E. Cárdenas
Text designer: Patrice Sheridan
This book was set in Adobe Caslon Pro and Whitney Condensed
by Alpha Design & Composition of Pittsfield, NH

10 9 8 7 6 5 4 3 2 1

Library of Congress Cataloging-in-Publication Data
Names: Gänsler, Franziska, 1987- author. |
Taylor, Imogen (Translator), translator.
Title: Eternal summer : a novel / Franziska Gänsler ;
translated from the German by Imogen Taylor.
Other titles: Ewig Sommer. English
Description: New York : Other Press, 2025.
Identifiers: LCCN 2024038795 (print) | LCCN 2024038796 (ebook) |
ISBN 9781635425260 (paperback) | ISBN 9781635425277 (ebook)
Subjects: LCGFT: Climate fiction. | Novels.
Classification: LCC PT2707.A56 E9513 2025 (print) |
LCC PT2707.A56 (ebook) | DDC 833/.92—dc23/eng/20241018
LC record available at https://lccn.loc.gov/2024038795
LC ebook record available at https://lccn.loc.gov/2024038796

Publisher's Note

This is a work of fiction. Names, characters, places, and incidents either are the
product of the author's imagination or are used fictitiously, and any resemblance
to actual persons, living or dead, events, or locales is entirely coincidental.

ETERNAL
SUMMER

1

The woman and child arrived on a Tuesday. It was weeks since I'd last had guests booked in. The trade fairs had been canceled or rescheduled because of the continuous state of alert, and there no longer seemed to be any other reasons to visit our region.

Although it was October, the past days' heat had stirred up the fires again. From the garden you could hear the helicopters circling the forest, and at two-hourly intervals, the announcements of the police as they patrolled the surrounding area: *Stay home, wear face masks, keep doors and windows shut. Stay home, wear face masks, keep doors and windows shut. Stay home.* They swelled and faded, came and went.

I'd been sunbathing and stood in the cool lobby in my dressing gown.

"Do you have a room available?"

It took some time for my eyes to adjust to the darkness and see them: a woman and a little girl. I put the girl at about three or four. The woman was around my age—mid, maybe late, thirties. She was wearing a light-colored dress with a purse over her shoulder and stood next to a small rolling suitcase, holding the child by the hand. I noticed that neither of them had a mask on, but maybe they'd been waiting for a while and had already put them away. Their legs and shoes were gray with dust; they'd brought the smell of the forest in with them, the smell of burned leaves and smoke.

I went ahead across the dining room, through the terrace doors, and into the garden. A low, wooden walkway in the style of a Japanese veranda led from the terrace to the bedrooms, past a fishpond and a small ornamental maple with brilliant red leaves. A young gray cat slinking through the stiff reeds stopped and stared at us.

Most guests were surprised by the garden. It wasn't in keeping with the rest of the hotel—the gloomy lobby, the old-fashioned dining room with its wooden furniture and dark-green curtains, the uninspired name, which was simply that of the town: Hotel Bad Heim. My grandfather had laid it out one summer while I was here with my mother, who loved all things Japanese. It was the summer before I started second grade. Now, all these years on, the garden was very much in step with the times; apart from the pond, it hardly needed water.

The sky was closing in from the forest. As we went along the walkway, I noticed that the woman had stopped behind me. I followed her gaze to the brown clouds piled up over the fire on the other side of the river, where the forest was almost entirely coniferous. Maybe, I thought, she hadn't been aware of the fires. Maybe she and the child had wound up here by chance. It must be an alarming sight to anyone not used to it, not expecting it, so I did my best to reassure her. "Don't worry," I said. "It's only the undergrowth burning. And there's a river in between. The flames can't cross that."

I unlocked the last door we came to, number five. The afternoon sun filtered through the closed shutters over the carpet and the bed.

The child had stayed in the garden and was watching the cat. The woman looked around and put her suitcase down next to the door. I asked if she'd like me to open the shutters. The room was the only one with a second window; it looked out over the field behind the house and up to the forest. The woman smiled at me.

I left the key on a small table. "You can eat here in the hotel," I said. "The restaurants in town are closed." I realized I'd forgotten to take her details. "Oh, and I'll need your names—and your IDs, please."

She nodded, smiling again. "Can I bring them to you later? I'm not sure where they are just now. We are Dorota and Ilya Ansel."

She spelled out the names for me, and I told her mine and said she should let me know if she needed anything. Then I left her to unpack. When I turned at the door, I saw that she had sat down on the bed and slipped off her shoes. The polite smile was gone. Instead, her face had a strained look, as though she'd begun to think of other things and hadn't expected me to look back.

I didn't see them again that day. I smoked, sunbathed, listened to music. In the evening I made myself a supper of canned tomatoes and sardines. I wondered whether to prepare something for the woman and child, but decided to wait. If they needed anything, I had enough for a simple meal: frozen fish, potatoes, bread, cheese, eggs—and plenty of cans.

I watched the news in the dining room. The unusual heat showed no sign of abating. No rain in sight. I'd opened the front door and the sliding door to the garden, and a warm breeze was wafting through the house. The never-ending summer brought with it a strange restlessness, a sense of powerlessness that most of the time I tried to ignore. It had to cool down sometime. Clouds would form; it would rain. The fall would come. A stubborn faith in an old normal, despite daily weather reports to the contrary. We stared helplessly at the temperature graph, at the red and blue lines representing day and night that remained unwaveringly high, unwaveringly close together. Each day brought the hope that the blue line, at least, would take a dive. The hope of cooler nights, of air masses colliding over the forest. The hope of clouds, of rain. Each day the *still*, the *not yet*. Each day the *sometime it'll break, it has to.* The waiting.

The endless summer not only fueled my fear of fires, it increased my sense of helplessness. I was used to fires in July and August, but we'd been waiting since mid-September for the air to clear and the earth to grow moist again.

I went on my usual round through the garden, fed the fish, chased off the cats, picked up the first fallen leaves from the pond. I could barely smell the burning anymore; the wind had turned and was coming from town. The fires would stop soon. It was a matter of days now.

I sat on one of the loungers, looking into the bright-pink sky, waiting until it was black on the horizon—until only the glow of the forest remained, far away on the other side of the river. I lit a cigarette and walked slowly over the gravel to the fence, beyond which the brown grass of the field stretched to the edge of the wood. I glanced at the room occupied by the woman and child. They hadn't come out since their arrival, and now it was dark in there behind the shutters—dark and silent. The television wasn't on, and no one was speaking. I realized I hadn't asked the woman how long they were intending to stay. One night, was my guess.

She must have a reason for staying here with her little girl at a time when there were so many restrictions and the air quality was so appalling. They were probably on their way somewhere; maybe they'd had to change trains, had gotten stranded. I imagined train tracks unable to cope with the heat, malfunctioning air conditioners, intolerably stuffy compartments.

I returned to my lounger, took my keys, and left the hotel by the main entrance. In the vestibule was a folded stroller that I hadn't noticed before.

The streets were empty. I walked slowly through town, past the windows taped with tinfoil, past the playground that had been closed since the summer to discourage outside play. A group of teenagers were sitting at the top of a jungle gym, smoking in a huddle, their faces reflecting the light from their phones—bright islands in the darkness. I heard them laugh. One of them grabbed a bar of the jungle gym and slowly pulled himself up. His gray back, his gray shoulders, rising and falling. He made it look easy, almost effortless.

I stopped at the crossroads for a moment, listening to the voices, the laughter, the bass, the weave of real sounds and cell phone noise. The traffic lights changed for no one; a train went through the empty station. Signs on the lampposts warned of the fires and the poor air quality, with illustrations to demonstrate correct procedure. Line drawings of heads in smoke masks, children and old people next to a thermometer, emergency numbers, a map showing muster stations in case of evacuation.

The warnings against outside activity had been in place since mid-April. The situation changed daily, depending on wind direction, the success of firefighting operations, the weather. Often the wind blew the smoke into town. Old people and children stayed home behind closed windows, watching maps of the area on their screens. Everyone kept an eye on the fluctuating zones of red, orange, and yellow that showed the levels of sulfur compounds in the air.

Bad Heim. Low-slung houses, paved front gardens, empty streets. Signposts to places that no longer existed: the spa, the casino, the vineyards. Billboards— and behind the billboards, public housing, a swath of white on the horizon like a range of mountains, balconies stacked over balconies, each private life separated from the next by a milk-glass partition. Scratching posts, birdhouses, plastic furniture with tablecloths clipped into place, clotheshorses, exercise bikes. The deserted bunker of the Grand Hotel, with its gappy sign jutting into the sky, its old curtains. A lot of the houses still bore traces of their former identity as bed-and-breakfasts—green signs with eternal promises of vacant rooms, relaxation, and fresh air.

I walked past the station, over the tracks, along the asphalt path. To the right of this path, after the last lamppost, was the field. From here you could see my hotel on the edge of town—the only hotel left in Bad Heim. The window of number five was a black oblong in the back of the building. The woman must have opened the shutters after all.

My little world lay in the bright circle of the outside lamp. Three loungers and a low table—and on the table, my speaker, my ashtray.

I crossed the field and slipped into the garden through a gap in the fence. When I was almost at the building I noticed a small, pale shape behind the window. It wasn't until it moved that I realized what I was looking at. The sole of a foot was being pressed against the glass by someone sitting there in the dark. A shudder ran through me. I'd assumed that the woman and child were asleep, but actually, it seemed, the woman was sitting at the window in the dark, looking out at the forest. She must be able to see me. I hurried past as if my thoughts were elsewhere, careful not to look her way. But the image of that foot lingered in my mind, strangely unpleasant—the pale toes, the ball, the heel, pressing against the glass as if to expand the room.

2

The next morning, the fields were coated in ash. Soft, gray flakes swirled in the corners of the garden, floated on the water. The sky was brown; low clouds loomed out of the forest. The wind had turned again in the night, but it was still blowing warm—too warm—and it had a bitter smell to it. I thought of the rescue workers calling out between the trees, shouting orders, their boots crunching over the forest floor.

The little girl, Ilya, was sitting alone in the garden when I came out of my room.

"You're up early." I smiled at her, but she only looked at me and went back to her game. She was poking the gravel with a short stick, stirring up ash and stones and burned leaves. I thought of the guidelines that advised against letting children spend too much time outside. I thought of the closed playgrounds, outdoor pools, and parks. But I didn't feel comfortable interfering. For years the only guests in the hotel had been people traveling on their own who appreciated being left in peace. Families didn't travel to fire-prone areas, and I had almost no experience of children. The few people I knew who'd become parents had moved away. Paula, Helene. I thought for a moment of calling my neighbor, Baby, to ask if there was anything I should look out for, but the girl seemed contented, absorbed in her game. It seemed unnecessary to disturb her or explain anything.

I inspected the maple as I did every morning, examining the red leaves for holes or little gray blisters, signs of heat damage, drought damage, smoke damage. It looked all right. I wondered again about letting the girl play outside and checked the app for that day's data. The levels weren't alarmingly high; Bad Heim and everything south of the river was in a pale-yellow zone. I decided that the standard precautions had been designed for permanent residents, for children who spent all day every day in and around fire-prone areas. One morning wouldn't harm the girl.

I told her I'd go and get breakfast, but she didn't react. In the kitchen I made coffee and hot milk, arranged sliced bread and little packets of jam and butter on two plates, put everything on a table by the window, fetched the high chair from the storeroom. I didn't have any fresh fruit, so I poured some canned fruit salad into a big glass bowl. Yellow, white, and orange chunks, garish red cherries in syrupy juice. Through the grimy windowpane I saw that the girl was still alone in the garden. The door to her mother's room was open a crack, which I hadn't noticed before. She was probably getting on with the packing, taking a shower, making the bed. I thought of the ash that would be sneaking in through that crack. Of the gray fuzz it would leave in the fibers of the carpet, in the sheets and towels. Later I would run the vacuum over the floor, plowing pale trails through the grime.

I drank my coffee at the kitchen door, smoked a cigarette, and ate the remains of a braided yeast loaf from the supermarket. Out here by the garbage cans, cats prowled, coming and going through the fence, squeezing their skinny bodies through the crevices.

By the time I went back into the garden, it was almost nine. The girl was sitting by the side of the pond, where red fish mouths broke the surface of the water, snapped at the ash as if it were food, and then vanished again. The water was too low, but now that restrictions were in force again I couldn't top it up more than once a week.

I sat down on a lounger near the child. I wondered if she was hungry or thirsty and thought about offering to bring her some breakfast, but she seemed very far away. After a while I got up to fetch the broom and swept my way along the veranda to number five. There seemed to be no sound coming from inside; I began to sweep more carefully. Through the crack in the door I could see only a few inches of room. A strip of carpet, the corner of the bed, and above it, motionless, the pale hollows of the woman's knees and her bent legs, one on top of the other. She must be lying with her back to the door without any covers, curled up like a small child.

Ash was lighter than ordinary dust. It had a habit of clinging, and when you brushed it off it immediately settled again. I quietly swept my way back to the other end of the veranda. A smoldering leaf drifted down in front of me and landed on the wooden balustrade. It had retained its curved shape, but between the black veins was nothing but white, burned-out cells. I propped the broom against the wall, carefully picked up the leaf, and carried it to the child, cupping it in my hands to protect it from the wind.

"Have you ever seen anything like it?" I crouched down next to the girl and slowly opened my fingers. She peered curiously into the hollow of my hand and inched a little closer. The leaf quivered there for a moment, like a butterfly, then the wind carried it away. It fell to dust a little way above our heads, vanished to nothing.

"Ilya!" The woman was standing in the crack in the door. She was wearing a white dress, and her hair was tied at the nape of her neck. "I'm sorry," she said to me, and then to her daughter: "Come on, Ilya, let Ms. Lehmann get on with her work."

I stood up and smiled. "It's fine, don't worry." I noticed that she was wearing the shoes she'd arrived in—that the straps were still gray with dust. She looked exhausted, as if she'd hardly slept.

The girl between us was still staring into the sky, looking for the vanished leaf.

"Would you like some breakfast, Mrs. Ansel?" I asked. "A cup of coffee?"

There was a slight lag in her response, as if the question had taken a moment to get through to her. Then she smiled at me, nodded, and came out, pulling the door shut behind her. The quick clack of her heels echoed on the wood.

When they were both sitting at a table, I closed the door to the terrace. The woman smoked, staring out at the forest. There was something nervous about her. Her toes and the corners of her mouth twitched like live wires. She scraped her forefinger over her thumb-nail, reached into space, swiveled her wrists. She hardly spoke to the girl, and though she smiled at me whenever I went over to take them something or clear something away, there was a certain reserve in her smile that told me it was a mere gesture of politeness—good manners rather than a desire to connect. This nervous tension in her reminded me of my mother, though she didn't have much else in common with her. The woman's eyes were an unusual color, somewhere between gray and green. She was tall and slender, and her face was all lines and angles—jaw, lips, cheekbones, eyebrows, part. She was unusually beautiful, but it was a beauty hemmed in by defenses; she avoided eye contact and moved as if she didn't want others to look at her. My mother had been soft, a shape that seemed to blur with its surroundings, always hungry for attention, affection, approval.

"Can I go make up your room?" I asked the woman when they had everything they needed.

"That's kind, but it won't be necessary."

I dusted the other tables, the backs of the chairs. Ash everywhere. "Do you know how long you'll be staying?"

She drew on her cigarette. "Not exactly," she said. "Is that all right?"

I explained that the hotel was empty anyway because of the fires, then followed her gaze over the garden and the field to the edge of the forest.

"There's really nothing to worry about," I said, smiling at the child. "The fires stay on the ground. The only thing here is the air—you know, when the wind's coming from the forest." I held up my duster, which was gray with ash. "It's just been too hot here for too long; the forest is dry." I shrugged. It was what people always said. I'd heard it so often—I was always saying it myself. I remembered that I was obliged to inform guests about the current situation: the risks, the rules, the protective measures. "Do you have masks? You'll need some if you want to be outside for any length of time." I fetched an information leaflet and two masks in plastic wrappers from reception. One for adults, one for children. "This tells you everything you need to know. The summer's been bad, but things will calm down again when the fall comes. When it rains."

The woman nodded and thanked me, taking the things I held out to her. She glanced at the leaflet, then put it down in front of her, along with the masks, and pushed her plate to one side, untouched. Her phone was lying next to her coffee cup; she picked it up, put it down, picked it up again. When the screen lit up I saw that someone was trying to call her. She turned it face down on the table.

When the little girl had finished her milk and had enough to eat, she was allowed to get down and go back into the garden. Her mother stayed at the table. The smell of smoke wafted in through the open door.

We watched the child, who was crouching by the pond again, running her fingers through the film of ash on the surface.

"Ilya thinks the ash is snow," the woman said with a short laugh, and I saw her face reflected in the window. She wasn't smiling. Her cigarette glowed; she inhaled, then blew smoke toward the glass. I noticed again how restless she was; she couldn't keep her hands still. A thin gold chain on her left wrist caught the sun, flashing glints of light onto the wall.

I tried to remember when we'd last had snow. It must have been five or six years ago—whole childhoods, I thought, without snow. The woman stubbed out her cigarette and rose to her feet, gathering up leaflet, masks, and phone. As I cleared the table I saw her sit down on one of the loungers. Ilya was blowing into the ash. I saw her laugh—saw the little flakes scatter across the water in front of her mouth.

In the days that followed, a routine established itself, but I saw little of either of them. I slept badly, coughing and sweating at night; I was often tired during the day. Every morning I woke early, hoping that the meteorologists had gotten it wrong and the weather had turned in the night, but they never had, and the heat persisted.

Sometimes Baby came to the fence, sweating profusely. She was thrilled there was someone new in town, not to mention someone with a child. Who were the mystery pair? Where had they come from and why didn't I have anything to report? She laughed and clapped me on the shoulder. We stood in the morning sun between the garden and the forest. Weather and fires unchanged. Then Baby made her way back home, along the path through the rough grass.

I checked my tree, fixed breakfast. If the wind was coming from town, I opened the doors and windows to get a breeze going. Then I sat in the garden with my coffee, smoking and reading until Ilya came out. She played by herself, looking at the fish or pushing little stones around. Sometimes she had a plastic figure with her, or a doll. I'd put some of my old toys out for her, buckets and spades, a little rake. It made me happy to see these things being used again. Ilya dug holes and shoveled gravel, and I heard her talking to herself, making up little scenes.

I noticed her watching me as I set about the daily chores of the hotel, and although we barely spoke, I liked the feeling of being less alone. Trailed by Ilya, I swept the veranda and wiped the ash off the chairs, tables, and loungers. At moments like these, the past overlaid the present. I remembered standing in the garden myself, staring at my aunt's hunched body, her serious face over swirls of soapy water. The stones under my bare feet and my mother next to me—her soft, white arms in the sun.

My mother had grown up in Bad Heim. She'd left home when she was sixteen, had me when she was twenty, died when she was thirty-two. When I was little I didn't understand why she hated it all so much: the hotel, Grandad, Auntie—everyone there except Baby. When Mom drove me to Bad Heim it was always on an impulse, always in a cloud of dust, always as a last resort. The nearer we got, the more restless she became. Darting eyes that didn't see me, fuchsia-nailed fingers gripping the wheel, long drags on slim cigarettes. For me it was the only place we ever went back to. Our suitcase on the back seat. Grandad waiting for me outside the hotel, lifting me in the air. Mom refusing to let him hug or kiss her, barely acknowledging him except for a weird smile. Weird and glassy, like everything about Mom when Grandad was around.

Maybe he thought we'd stay if he did a good job of the garden, but the only place that existed for my mother in Bad Heim was the station. The station and the sky.

That summer before second grade, old illustrated books and travel guides were piled up next to the ashtray on Grandad's table in the dining room. He studied them through the smoke of his cigarettes, a pair of murky glasses perched on his nose. Local men came by to put up a canopy, hammer in posts, lay the walkway. Grandad stood in the sun in his undershirt and dug a hole in the middle of the garden for the pond.

The lawn, the vegetable patch, the swings—all that had been cleared away. A load of gravel was delivered, and Grandad leveled it himself, one stroke at a time with a big rake. He paced slowly up and down through the dirt, covering the soil with a layer of stones, a pattern of furrows—around the hole, around the tiny new maple. The fish came last of all.

My mother lolled around by the window or in the garden in her yellow kimono, smoking, talking on the phone, writing her diary. She watched Grandad as if none of it had anything to do with her.

I stood at a distance. I remember feeling sorry for Grandad. I remember his skinny old arms and the suitcase that Mom and I never unpacked; we'd simply take out what we needed every day and put it back again later, straight from the clothesline.

Weeks that edged into fall, Mom's growing listlessness as she lay on the lounger or in bed—at some point it had become hard for her to raise a cigarette to her mouth or a comb to her hair, to hold a mirror in one hand and a lipstick in the other. Shaky red or fuchsia smudged over her beautiful lips. Things that slipped from her fingers to the floor, books and glasses that lay there till Grandad or Auntie or Baby or I picked them up. Broken glass, cigarette burns. Baby washing and cutting my mother's hair, blond curls on the carpet.

Mom saying, "Should've hanged myself years ago." To her reflection, to her sister, to me. Baby, who was the only one who'd been able to laugh about it.

Baby, who was still around today. Who loved the thrill and drama of the forest fires—anything to keep boredom at bay. We were hanging in there, Baby and I.

After the garden chores I went on my rounds through the four empty guest rooms. My apartment was on the other side of the garden, next to the storeroom and the place where I kept garden tools, loungers, parasols, things like that. A door marked *Private* led to two rooms and a small bathroom. At first my grandparents had lived there alone; then Mom and Auntie had come along. Later it was just Grandad and the girls, then Grandad and Auntie, and eventually he and I. Now that the hotel was almost always empty I was hardly ever in the apartment. I slept in one of the rooms and used the bathroom, but other than that I spent my time in the empty communal rooms, which I had gradually made my own.

While I vacuumed, aired the beds, and dusted, Ilya stayed in the garden. Sometimes she stopped in the middle of her game, and if I noticed her looking my way I smiled at her. Now and then I explained to her why some chores had to be done and others had to wait. That the bedding could be aired only when the wind was coming from town. That the laundry had to be dried inside. That the pond was filled once a week.

"Would you like to help me?" I asked, and to my surprise she nodded and came closer. I gave her a basket full of miniature bars of soap, and together we exchanged the unused packets in the bathrooms for new ones.

Baby came over the field to the fence and waved at us.

"Busy doing nothing again, huh?" she called out, as she always did, laughing her smoker's laugh, and she took a soft chocolate from her apron pocket and put it on one of the fence posts for Ilya, who stood on the veranda, basket in hand, looking from Baby to the chocolate and back again.

"Come get it before the critters find it." Baby had gray teeth, a gold chain on her soft skin, a greasy old face mask slung under her chin. She was too bulky to squeeze through the gap in the fence.

I was always glad to see her. With her, everything came straight to the surface—every thought that passed through her sweating head, every memory. Baby lived alone in the house next door; she'd grown up with my grandfather and been in and out of the hotel all her life. She came to help out when Grandma died—took my mother and aunt to school, cleaned rooms, served in the restaurant. She brought food and watched TV with me when my aunt died soon after Mom, and I was left on my own in the hotel with Grandad. She helped me change his diapers when he still had his full body weight and I wasn't strong enough to turn him over. Later, when I knew how, it was easy—when I knew that I had to start by pulling out the wet sheet from underneath him and putting on a clean one, then undo his diaper, soak his dirty skin, wipe it, dry it, powder it. His body was thin by then, surprisingly light and defenseless. These days Baby's help tended to take the form of good advice. Sin's a matter between you and God. Oral sex requires stamina, not love. Warm prosecco is the best cure for headaches, cognac for nausea, slivovitz for period pain. Every malady had its antidote in Baby's liquor cabinet.

As I approached, I could smell her over the fence and through the smoke—her warm body and the chicken thigh that she was sucking on. Scraps of white meat clung to her tongue when she licked the grease from her fingers. We looked at the sky, the forest. Baby knew everything that was going on in town, but it wasn't a lot. Everyone was lying impassive under the perpetual sun. Everyone was waiting for the rain.

We could hear the sirens, and sometimes, far away, firefighting planes circled through the smoke. That meant the fires were growing higher, harder to control.

It was Baby who drew my attention to the birds. "The critters still gather, but they don't migrate anymore." Hundreds of starlings, like pepper over the dry field, rising and falling in a cloud, scattering, regrouping in a threadbare strip, circling against the yellow sky, their cries and beating wings soundless to us.

Ilya joined us at the fence and stared raptly into the sky. Her mother was in their room, and I wondered if she was standing at the window—if, in that moment, we were all looking at the same thing.

Baby waved her bare chicken bone in the air and pointed out the predator with a laugh, a big bird that flew into the flock from above or below, making it change shape. "What a fucking mess we're in," she cried, but she sounded happy, as though cheered by the sinister image of birds fleeing the burning forest.

Mrs. Ansel emerged from the room. Baby gave her a nod and I called out, "Good morning."

She returned our greetings politely and beckoned to Ilya. We watched them head for the dining room.

"Run away from a man, she has," Baby said, laughing and coughing. "I can feel it in my guts."

"Why do you think that?" I asked, but Baby was already walking away and only waggled her head and waved.

After breakfast in the dining room, the woman and Ilya usually went back to their bedroom. If I was in the garden I would hear the TV through the door— the shower, the flush of the toilet. In the late afternoon they often left the hotel for an hour or two. The woman put Ilya in the stroller; they both wore masks, and the woman wore sunglasses. She didn't tell me where they went and I didn't ask, but once—it must have been the Saturday after they arrived, because I was driving back from the wholesale store—I spotted them on the side of the road. The woman was wearing the same light-colored dress she'd had on when she arrived. She was pushing the stroller and walking fast. It seemed strange to me that she'd walked all that way in her flimsy high heels, pushing Ilya along the highway, through the gray air, half on the asphalt and half on the bumpy shoulder. I slowed the car; she stared ahead and quickened her pace. I let down the passenger window, called, "Would you like a lift?" But she seemed not to hear; she didn't react. She hurried on, hands gripping the stroller, eyes fixed ahead, shoes slapping her heels at every step. I rounded the bend and pulled over into the next park- ing space to wait, but they didn't appear. I got out and started to walk back toward them. There was no fork in the road—just the highway and, on either side, clus- ters of dry trees, rough bushes, garbage. My guests were nowhere to be seen. I returned to the car and a few minutes later I headed home.

It was late when they arrived back at the hotel. I was sitting in the dining room watching TV, my concern growing. The air pollution on the other side of the river was high; it had been climbing steadily all day. I was afraid something had happened, afraid the woman had passed out from walking so fast, breathing through her mask. I imagined all kinds of things. I thought about calling Baby—maybe she'd heard something. Then, just as I'd decided to retrace my path along the highway, they showed up. Ilya was crying. The woman was carrying her in one arm and pushing the stroller with the other. They came across the parking lot, their arms and legs pale in the lurid light. I held the door open, took the stroller from the woman. She looked exhausted, her eyes red; I wondered if she'd been crying or if it was the air. Inside, still holding the child, she sat down at the table where they had breakfast every morning.

"Could we have a bite to eat maybe? And something to drink? Please."

Ilya was snuggled up to her mother, crying, her face buried in the woman's blond hair. I brought juice for her and mineral water for her mother. Then I went into the kitchen. I felt somehow responsible for the situation. Maybe I should have warned them when I saw them going out. Should have alerted them to the air quality.

I threw vermicelli into a pan of broth, broke two eggs into it, put two bowls and a bread basket on a tray. When

I returned to the dining room the girl had fallen asleep on her mother's shoulder. The juice glass was empty. The woman sat in the lamplight in front of the black windowpane; behind her, a dim glow came from the forest.

I put the bowls of soup on the table, and she lit a cigarette and blew the smoke out of the side of her mouth, away from the child's little face.

"It was stupid of me, I didn't take anything to drink." She gave me a narrow-lipped smile. I smiled back. "I didn't think we'd be out that long."

"Did you get lost?"

She shook her head vaguely. Between drags on her cigarette she took small spoons of soup from one of the bowls.

"Did I see you on the highway?" I asked. "Is that possible?"

She gave a sudden laugh, and everything in her face changed. For the first time I saw that one of her front teeth was shorter than the others, two or three millimeters shorter. I was surprised I hadn't noticed before, and wondered if she consciously hid the uneven teeth—if she'd trained herself to smile in a particular way, so that the short tooth didn't show unless she lost control of her face.

"I drove past you, but you didn't hear me."

She was still laughing. Her daughter's head jiggled, and the woman stroked her fine hair. Again I was reminded of my mother—the mischievous twist to her mouth that seemed somehow incongruous on her face.

"I'm sorry," the woman said. "I thought you were someone else."

"You could have called the hotel," I said. "I'd have come to fetch you."

"Oh, thank you, that's very kind. But I didn't have my phone on me."

Ilya opened her eyes sleepily. "Soon, soon," the woman whispered, stroking her head again. "We'll go to bed soon." But she made no move to get up. I wondered who she'd thought I was, whom she knew in the area.

"It was stupid of me. Walking all that way without a phone and with nothing to eat or drink. But thank you for your offer."

She pointed at the second bowl of soup. "Would you like to join me, Ms. Lehmann? Ilya's too sleepy to eat."

Although I'd already eaten, I accepted. We sat and ate, then smoked a cigarette or two. The forest gleamed in the distance, but I could no longer hear any planes or helicopters. We talked a little, then sat in silence, looking out the window into the darkness, through our silhouetted reflections. The woman stroked the sleeping child on her lap. They seemed alone in the world.

When I got up and began to clear the dishes, she stubbed out her cigarette and rose carefully with Ilya in her arms. I helped her through the glass door, then followed her into the garden and switched on the outside lamp. We said whispered good nights to each other, but when I saw her struggling to get into her room with the girl in her arms I hurried after her, took the key from her hand, and unlocked the door. A sour, stale smell poured out. In the oblong of light cast by the garden lamp was a mess of clothes, scrawled paper, tights, torn wrappers, odd children's shoes. None of it was in keeping with the woman's well-groomed appearance.

She picked her way through the things and put the girl down on the big double bed. As I whispered good-bye again and made to leave, I heard her say something I didn't catch. I turned to her.

"These are very strange times," she repeated. She had come to the door. I waited for an explanation, but she only smiled wanly.

"Yes," I said, thinking of the forest fires. "For all of us."

"Yes, of course," she said. Then she wished me good night and closed the door.

Later, lying in bed, I thought of her. I saw her pushing the stroller, two wheels on the road, two on the steep, gravelly shoulder. Her elegantly shod feet, her white back, her blond hair, her clenched hands. I saw her mask and sunglasses covering all her face except her forehead, temples, cheekbones. Everything about her intent on the road ahead.

3

The next day, the first call came. It was early morning, and as far as I could tell, the woman and child were still asleep. When I picked up, a man called Alexander Vargas asked if I had rooms available. I pointed out that there was a hospitality ban in force because of the fires. In fact, like so many of the regulations in the region, the rule was easily bent and open to interpretation. Strictly speaking, all it said was that you couldn't take bookings through online portals, via email, or by phone. If someone simply turned up at the hotel and asked for a room, as the woman had done, the ban didn't apply.

Now that there was no longer any tourism in the region and the trade fairs had been rescheduled, most hotels were closed anyway. When people called, I usually explained that although I could no longer take reservations over the phone, the hotel was open and practically empty. It didn't happen often. The occasional guest still came here for a wedding or a funeral, but even that was getting rarer.

"You're saying the hotels in Bad Heim aren't taking guests just now?" the man asked. "I wouldn't get a room if I was traveling in the area?"

I had no reason not to mention the loophole, but I didn't. Maybe I was worn out by the heat, the continuing fires, the sleepless nights. Maybe, over the long summer, I'd gotten used to the emptiness of the hotel, the calm of a routine that didn't require me to adjust myself to other people's rhythms. I'd only just settled into a new normal with the woman and child. I liked the sameness of our days and the margin of overlap between my life and theirs. The thought of taking in someone else was too much.

I spoke of the fires, the hazards. "You should avoid the area if possible," I said.

"But it's not good for you either."

"We're used to it," I replied. "Things pick up again in the winter. Some of the trade fairs have been rescheduled; they haven't all moved away."

"I meant healthwise," he said. "I'm sorry, I'm a doctor. It's a professional tic."

I laughed. I began to wonder if I shouldn't offer to take him in after all. I thought of the forty-eight euros I charged for a single room, breakfast included. I was just telling myself that people traveling alone made very little extra work when he said goodbye and hung up. Maybe he had a funeral to attend, I thought. Now that the fires were in the news again, people came only if they had good reason, things that couldn't wait.

The protests, the press—all that happened on the other side of the river. I saw the glow of the fire on TV, the low burn that followed the rise and fall of the forest floor in a greedy, smoldering line—and beyond, over the treetops, the purple sky.

White, brightly lit faces in clean white masks summed up developments, straining their voices over the fire and the sirens, speaking loud and clear into the camera, wanting to get out quick.

My attention was caught by the young protesters at the right edge of the picture. A small group, an anonymous chorus barely audible over the general din—but I knew what they were shouting. "What do we want? Climate justice! When do we want it? Now!"

Behind them, in the background, was the climate camp they'd set up at the edge of the forest, the tents and banners pulsing in the blue light of the fire trucks and ambulances, coming and going, coming and going.

I paused the picture and studied their blue, glowing faces in the silence, their open mouths. I knew where the camp was, knew the hiking trail that led past it, recognized the wayside cross donated by the local savings bank. I tried to square my memory of the place with the present. It was all so close. The river was only a little way behind them—behind the young protesters, the reporters, and the emergency workers, behind the trees and the fire. And just on the other side of the river came the deciduous forest and the field. The fence, the garden, my hotel.

I hit play again and went back to watching the news. A reporter was standing in front of the activists' tents. One of the young protesters was speaking into the microphone that the reporter held out to her. She made a connection between what was happening in the forest and global upheavals, spoke of a time of multiple crises, and painted a gloomy picture in which areas like ours became uninhabitable. I looked at her eyes above the face mask, her short hair. Her forehead gleamed in the floodlight, her gray shirt was damp at her chest and under her arms. The reporter asked what had motivated her to come to the forest.

"We're here because these fires are human-made, and that has to stop."

That *we* echoed in my head. Other activists had gathered behind the girl; I counted seven. They stood silent during the interview, silent in front of the loud forest, gazing intently into the camera, holding their banners. The short-haired woman spoke for them all. Then the reporter thanked her, and the group began to chant again, a furious round that seemed to chase itself in circles: *What do we—when do we—justice—now.*

I wondered how many seconds' lag there was between real time in the forest and the live broadcast—
how long it took for the activists' chants to reach my
TV. A strange emptiness filled the silent dining room. I
envied the protest group their sense of belonging, their
faith in each other and in their cause. Compared with
them I felt numb with loneliness.

Although I realized that the images on TV were of
direct concern to me, the hotel, Bad Heim, and although
I knew that everything here would only get worse—that
fall no longer existed and winter was only a brief respite
that grew briefer with every year—I had the impression
that the activists and reporters were talking about something else. Although I could see the fire through the
window, the situation in the forest eluded me. My deal-
ings with the fire were limited to wiping up the fly ash,
keeping my little world in order.

Everyone who could had moved away, most of them
in that second summer, when two men had lost their
lives in the forest and a public awareness campaign had
warned of respiratory diseases and cancer. Only people
like me had stayed, people without children who couldn't
imagine living anywhere else. Everything I owned was
here, and a lot of others were in the same boat. They had
houses and gardens. For most people in Bad Heim, life
was something you were born into, inextricably bound
up with place and community. And as long as the fires
didn't cross the river, there was no direct threat. There

were no attacks, no persecution, no starvation. Nothing to make us leave. We had long, dry summers, and some said there had always been forest fires—it was just that there'd been more important things to worry about in the world. Some said that real estate prices had been deliberately driven down, that there were already zoning plans for the land, that our property had already been redistributed by third parties. They saw the fires as a plot to smoke us all out. The longer the situation continued the more it became a question of faith, with theories and so-called evidence on either side. For my part I believed neither the gossip nor the conspiracy theories. I knew that what the geo-ecologists, meteorologists, and climate activists were saying was true. Not that it made any difference. I had no way of influencing the situation. Like a piece in a board game, I kept an eye on developments, tending to the little square that was my life one move at a time. I played by the rules, I followed instructions, and so far there had been no need to leave.

Five or six years ago, when the fires had suddenly intensified, I'd had a lot of reporters and photographers staying in the hotel. They'd interviewed people and taken photos: children standing at the fence with yellow smoke billowing over their soft hair; old people in masks, staring grimly from their balconies at the strange, black countryside unrolling on the far side of the river; injured birds, injured cats, injured deer. When the fall came, bringing rain, all that stopped. Then in the spring it started again, a little earlier each year: the hazard signs, the police announcements, the maps with their shifting zones of yellow and red. The constantly updated warning apps that we were soon checking as a matter of course. Yellow meant vigilance; orange, lockdown; red, evacuation. The summers here hovered between yellow and orange. Masks, wind, ash, watering eyes, sore throats, closed parks and pools, cordoned-off playgrounds. Leaves that burned in the air and floated down to the hot gravel. All this against a backdrop of smoldering brush across the river.

Three days later the man called a second time. I'd only just gotten up. It was six o'clock. He told me his name again and apologized for calling me back, especially at such an early hour.

"I'm afraid the situation hasn't changed," I said.

There was a strange silence.

"I'm sorry to bother you again," he repeated. "It's just—" He broke off and fell silent once more. "The thing is, I'm looking for someone, and your hotel is my only lead."

I said nothing.

"I know this must sound weird, but I'm looking for my wife and daughter."

I took a deep breath. Baby's words came back to me. *Run away from a man, she has.*

"Where do I come into this?" I asked evasively.

"My wife mentioned your town in a conversation," he said vaguely. "And yours seems to be the only hotel that's still open." When I said nothing, he went on, "I know what you're thinking. But I've already looked everywhere else. She isn't with friends or family; she isn't anywhere."

"Your wife told you she was coming here? To Bad Heim?"

"She mentioned the place to someone. This was a few days ago. She'd been away with our daughter and should have come back—to Berlin—but she's disappeared without a trace. Isn't where she was and hasn't come home either."

I said nothing.

"Legally speaking, it's kidnapping. That's why I'm trying to find her myself, do you understand? I've done some research, and apparently people who go missing never pick a place entirely at random. There's always some clue. In their biography, in the things they've read or seen or heard. Do you understand? The police follow the same procedure."

I felt he was going too far; he sounded like a commentator in a documentary, a true crime show. I was tempted to laugh, but something in his voice told me he was serious.

"Have you reported your wife missing?" I asked, since he'd mentioned the police. "Something might have happened to her."

"No," he said hesitantly. "I'm sure she went away with our daughter voluntarily. Her phone was still on for the first few days. I could see she was online. She got my messages and calls; she just didn't answer them. Now it's switched off."

I remembered the woman's phone on the table, saw her pick it up and turn it over. She hadn't had it with her the day she walked down the highway. I'd never seen her on a call.

I said nothing. There was something desperate about the early hour of the man's call, the painstaking detail of his account. He hasn't slept, I thought, and I imagined a man sitting up all night in an empty apartment, brooding, trawling the internet, waiting for morning to come so he could call me. There was nothing unpleasant about his voice, but I knew that didn't mean anything. I thought of domestic violence stats, of articles I'd read— of Baby, who'd seen it in the woman a mile off. I must tell her about this, I thought, ask her if I should tell the woman about the man's calls. Baby would grasp the situation; she'd know what to do. I felt the menace in the man's words: *kidnapping, the police.* Like stones making ripples. Uncontrollable repercussions. Drama I didn't want to be involved in. I tried to end the conversation.

"I'm afraid I can't help you," I said.

He didn't give up. "Maybe someone's called you? About a room?"

"Only you," I said.

He thanked me, calm and polite to the end, and asked if he could give me his number and would I let him know if a woman called, if anyone tried to book a room.

I noted his name and number on a piece of paper. *Alexander Vargas.* It occurred to me that the woman had never shown me her ID. I wondered whether to ask the man for the names of his wife and child to make sure he was talking about the same people, but I decided not to bother. First, the woman might have given me fake names, and second, I was afraid of giving myself away if I spoke to him much longer. I assured him I'd get in touch if a woman called. Then I wished him luck and hung up.

I took a cup of coffee into the garden and sat down in the sun, which wasn't so strong at that time of day. I lit a cigarette. The little gray cat was picking its way through the reeds to the pond. I shooed it away.

It was going to be another hot day. The sky hung low over the woods, but the wind was coming from town and blew in warm gusts over the field and pond. The maple was swaying, its red leaves spinning through the air toward the forest. I imagined the situation there changing with the wind—orders being yelled, reporters and activists being moved on by the fire brigade, having to regroup. I thought of the girl with the short hair. I imagined tents and banners being packed up in a hurry, the protesters toiling through the forest, keeping an eye on one another.

Everyone here was familiar with the diagrams. A cross to mark the position of the fire brigade, a blue arrowhead to represent the fire driven by the wind, and along the sides of this arrow—the red zones. No one who was in these zones when the wind changed could escape the fire on foot. It was here that the two men had been caught by the flames—the men whose deaths had brought the fires to the attention of the international media. I don't know why there was no talk of zones or wind direction before—maybe the fires hadn't been as intense, maybe people were just lucky. Before those men died, the fire was seen as a local problem—a new phenomenon, to be sure, but part of the natural succession of the forest. A result of the hot summer, the drought. Over when fall came. We didn't even have words for what was happening. It was only afterward that people started talking about the *dead man zone*, a term that would change our perception of what was going on in the forest.

On TV, the area was generally shown from above, filmed by a drone. The fire, seen through the smoke, and beyond the fire, the flattened forest. Fallen trees, black on gray. The river a dark strip, deep and wide, a trench splitting the forest in two.

It was not unthinkable, of course, that the fire would leap onto our side of the river, or that fire would break out here too. But so far it hadn't happened. The trees on our side were deciduous, which meant they stored more moisture and didn't burn as easily. The general view was that as long as the fire stayed on the ground, this side of the river was safe.

When I'd finished my coffee I put the cup down on the low table and walked through the garden to the fence. Ilya was nowhere to be seen; the door to number five was shut, the shutters closed.

The air was less dense than in previous weeks; it felt soft and smooth in my throat. I looked out over the field. It was thick with starlings right to the edge of the forest—fist-sized black bodies pecking at the brown grass, thrusting their beaks into the hard soil. I wasn't sure there was anything left to find in the dry ground.

I slipped through the gap in the fence. The birds grew agitated. They stalked off, putting space between them and me, or fluttered into the air and landed a safe distance away.

In the forest, the branches fanned up, yellow and brown, closing overhead to form bright roofs. Smoke hung in the trees like mist, out of reach of the wind. Despite the early hour it was warm—a strange warmth that had nothing to do with the weather. A warmth that smelled of burned weeds, burned leaves, burned earth.

I heard a rustle. It was closer than the fires and didn't sound like an acorn or chestnut bouncing off leaves and trunks on its way to the ground. A bird, I thought, a deer—but the branches hung still, and no animal started away when I moved. I followed the narrow path that led to the river.

The water lay smooth between the trees, black at its shady edges and gray in the middle, with ash that blew over from the far bank. I remembered the river before the fires, when it was still clear—the sky reflected in the water, bright autumn leaves patterning the surface. Now the surface was dull and dusty. Feathers and dark leaves floated motionless on a film of ash. I remembered the feeling of stepping into it as a child. The sudden coolness at the edge of the forest, as if you'd walked into a house. The clear, earthy forest air. The mud squelching beneath your bare feet as you sank in. The cold that lurked beneath the warm surface, even in the hottest weeks of the summer. My grandfather waiting at the edge, stripped to the waist, his trousers rolled up to his knees. His soft old body. Afterward, when I got out of the water, he would press me to his chest to warm me, whether I liked it or not.

I dipped my hand into the river, expecting it to be as cold as in my childhood, but the water was warm—warmer than my hand. The smell of burning hung in the air.

Again I heard a noise—a splash, a voice. A few yards upstream, a tree had fallen lengthwise into the river, and there at the water's edge, with a long, wet stick in her hand, was Ilya, poking the mud and talking softly to herself, as I'd often seen her do in the garden. I stood up and looked around for her mother, but there was no sign of her; the child seemed to be alone. I called her name and hurried toward her. It was a shock to see her here, alone by the water in the forest, in this burned-smelling air. She looked at me, her eyes wide; she hadn't noticed me until now. I stopped a little way from her.

"Hey." I smiled at her. She was wearing short pajamas and little leather slippers, and her legs and slippers were wet and muddy. "Are you out all by yourself?"

Ilya turned to the river again, then shook her head and went back to poking with her stick. Her little form was dimly reflected in the water. As she prodded the surface, the image blurred—her white pajamas, the sun on her chest, her skinny arms. Small burrs and thistles clung to her hair and her pant legs. I was reminded of the scrawny cats that skulked around the hotel. They had the same hesitancy, the same alert stillness, their ears pricked toward me, even as they pretended to ignore me.

I hunkered down next to her. "Are you lost?" I asked.

She was silent, but her eyes moved to the water, searching my reflection. I smiled again—a milky, crooked smile, hardly visible.

Then she said something, but so quickly and quietly that I didn't understand. The only word I heard was *Mommy.*

"Are you looking for your mommy?" I asked, and she nodded.

I'd heard of children sleepwalking. Maybe that would explain why she was roaming the forest at the crack of dawn.

"Isn't your mommy in the hotel?"

Ilya stared at the water and said nothing. I waited. The situation worried me. The forest, the water, the air—especially the air. I stood up. "Would you like to help me in the hotel again?" I asked, but she didn't stir. For a while we stood together, between the bushes at the edge of the river. It was peaceful. Only the smell and the heat drifted across from the fires on the other side. I couldn't leave Ilya here, but neither could I pick her up and carry her off.

"Shall I tell you a story?" I asked. I remembered a series of stories my mother had made up for me about two sisters in a magic forest who'd run away from home. When I was little I'd imagined the forest of Bad Heim as the backdrop for these stories—the mysterious, dark-green world that began just behind the hotel. I started to tell Ilya one, and with every sentence I remembered names and details I hadn't thought of for years. Toya and Soya, the sisters; Pijou, the little talking dog who went everywhere with them; the magic bazaar run by bugs. I watched Ilya as I spoke. She was standing very still, listening. I walked a little way, hoping she'd follow of her own accord.

"Come on," I said brightly when she didn't move. "I'll tell you the rest of the story on the way."

Ilya slowly shook her head, staring at the other side of the river, where the trees vanished into the smoke only a few rows into the forest. I couldn't imagine that her mother had walked into the burning forest and left her behind, but Ilya must have seen something—or must think she'd seen something.

"We can't cross here," I said. "It gets quite deep in the middle." Ilya stared at the still water in front of her, warm and murky at her feet. Her mouth had narrowed, as if she doubted my words or her own intentions— doubted that she could cross the river, or that she had a chance of finding her mother on the other side.

"Will you come back with me?" I asked, and when she didn't reply, I added, "If your mommy's not in the hotel, we'll go look for her in my car." I hadn't actually planned that far, but I was expecting—or hoping— that her mother would be in the hotel, that she'd still be asleep, that I could get Ilya back before she noticed she was missing. I walked on, and to my relief, I heard little footsteps behind me, the crackle of dry leaves under leather soles. I waited until Ilya had caught me up. "Would you like to hear what happens next?"

We walked back together, and I told her about Toya and Soya crawling through a tunnel into the magic forest, finding a shoe inhabited by the king of the mice, and rescuing the king from being eaten by Pijou. When we came to the field the starlings had gone.

In the garden, my empty cup was still on the table and Ilya's mother's door was still closed. Her window was closed too. I imagined the gray room behind the shutters, the thin lines cast through the slats by the yellow morning light—onto the carpet, the coverlet, a sleeping arm.

I was wondering whether to knock or get the girl some breakfast first, or at least something to drink, when the terrace door slowly opened at the other end of the garden. I saw the woman's long fingers, then her blond head, her shoulders. Her shoes were tucked under her right arm. She stepped onto the terrace barefoot and quietly closed the door behind her.

"Mommy!" Ilya skipped past me over the gravel. I saw the woman start and spin round. She hadn't seen us, hadn't been expecting us. Wherever she'd come from, she had clearly hoped to remain unnoticed. But she immediately collected herself. Smiled, bent down, put her shoes on the ground, held out her arms to her daughter. By the time I reached the terrace, the woman's face was buried in the child's hair, and the girl was squeezed into a crooked embrace.

I went into the dining room and began to take down the stiff sheets and covers that I'd hung up to dry. I remembered that I'd been meaning to offer to do the woman's laundry. So far she'd refused to let me clean her room, only asking once for a change of towels.

"You're up early," I heard through the french door. "Were you looking for me?" Through the glass I saw her stand up. She looked worn out; the face mask had left a dark furrow around her nose and mouth. "Are you hungry?"

I heard Ilya reply, but didn't catch what she said.

"I need a quick shower. Will you come with me or would you rather stay here?" She plucked thistles out of Ilya's hair as she spoke. "What have you been up to?" The woman picked up her shoes, and she and Ilya walked back along the wooden veranda to their room, Ilya leaning against her mother's legs, clinging to her hand.

Where had the woman been?

I went into the kitchen and started to fix breakfast for them. I fried eggs, bacon, and a tomato; I put bread in the toaster. I laid the table in the dining room. It was eight o'clock. The morning news was on TV. Election results, grain shortage, fleeing people, sports, weather. It was still too hot, no prospect of rain.

When they reappeared, I took them coffee and warm milk.

"Would you mind switching that off?" the woman asked with a cautious smile. "I hated it even as a child."

"Really? You hated TV?" I looked for the remote control. "I thought all kids loved TV. I was glued to the screen 24/7." I laughed, but switched off the television. The room fell quiet.

"Just the news," she said. "I still can't stand it."

She was looking more relaxed; the red lines under her eyes had almost vanished. Her hair was wet, and she'd changed into jeans and a blouse. Ilya had changed too; she was wearing a yellow dress and sandals instead of her pajamas and muddy slippers. I put the food on the table.

"I hope she didn't give you any trouble," the woman said. Ilya grabbed a slice of toast and crammed it into her mouth. Her mother put bacon and eggs on a plate for her; she herself only drank coffee.

I was wondering whether to tell her I'd found Ilya in the forest when she said, "I went for a little walk. I didn't want to wake Ilya."

She must have left the hotel before I woke, before the man called. I imagined her sneaking off through the garden at dawn, wandering the empty streets. I imagined Ilya waking alone in the room and setting off through the starlings to the forest to look for her mother. I looked down at the child, at her soft little hands on the table, and felt retrospective panic at the thought that I might not have gone into the forest that morning.

The woman interrupted my thoughts. "Do you happen to know if there's a local history museum here? Or maybe an archive? I'd like to know what it was like here when it was still a spa town." I remembered what the man on the phone had said about his wife mentioning Bad Heim. "The clientele, the atmosphere. It must have changed an awful lot."

In a cabinet at reception there was a box of postcards from the days when my grandfather had run the hotel. The postcards were all the same—a black-and-white photograph of my grandparents on a bench at the hotel entrance. My grandfather had his arm around Grandma and she was leaning against him. They were both very smartly dressed. She was wearing a full-skirted summer dress and high heels, her black hair set in tight waves around her face. He wore a white shirt and a hat. They looked cheerful, welcoming. In the sky, in curly, old-fashioned writing, it said: *Greetings from Lovely Bad Heim.*

I remembered "Lovely Bad Heim" from my childhood. The town had been a different place; the hotel too. At the time when the photo was taken, it had been a popular destination for artists of all kinds. My grandfather had often talked of those times. Evenings that went on long into the night. My grandmother painting, my mother singing to the guests as a little girl. There were pictures of that too.

I went and fetched one of the postcards and gave it to the woman. She ran her finger over the faces. Then she flashed a smile at me. "Is that your grandmother? You look so alike."

I laughed and shook my head. My grandmother had been famous for her beauty. People in town still talked about it, still raved about her to me sometimes. She'd died young, when my mother and aunt were little.

The woman continued to look at me, as if she were seeing me for the first time. "Don't you think?" she said.

I shook my head again. "I take after my father's side more." Her gaze was beginning to embarrass me; I was conscious of my high forehead, my thin hair, my bony body. "My mother looked like her," I said. "She was blonde, but she had the same face, the same build."

The woman was still staring at me. "You have a fine face," she said, and looked from me to the postcard and back again, comparing.

I heard myself laugh incredulously again, heard the defensiveness in my voice as I said, "I was once told I wouldn't be beautiful until someone fell in love with me as a human being."

"What a strange thing to say." She laughed and shook her head. For a moment, I thought, we had crossed the border separating us as strangers; we had spoken more intimately than our relationship warranted. We looked at each other, then I turned away. It had been a long time since I'd felt anything like this, but I recognized the thrill, the possibility of attraction between us.

She tapped a corner of the postcard against the table. "I've read a lot about the town and what it used to be like here. That's why I'm interested."

I wasn't surprised. Bad Heim was often mentioned in novels and poems, and always as a haven, an oasis. There were some old photo albums from that time in the hotel. Pictures that Grandad had taken and compiled. When I offered to find them for the woman sometime, she seemed pleased.

"If you like," I said, turning to Ilya, "you can come with me and see if you can find some toys."

I thought of the ceiling-high stacks of boxes in my apartment. The relics of old Bad Heim, the dresses, coats, and shoes, the dollhouse, the building blocks.

Odds and ends that had belonged to my grandparents, my aunt, my mother. Somewhere among those things were the picture albums.

The phone rang, and I left Ilya and the woman and went to sort out a delivery of bed linen I had ordered. When I returned to the dining room it was empty except for the dirty dishes on the table. The twisted cigarette butts and the rim of the woman's glass were bright pink from her lipstick.

4

I spent the day sealing cracked tiles. Things withstood the heat only to an extent; they expanded, trying to find space where there was none. Ilya was playing in the garden; her mother was sitting in the shade, reading. After a while I heard Baby strike up a conversation with her over the fence. I listened to the laughter, the laconic replies. I thought of Ilya in the forest. Of the caller. When Baby's questions grew more insistent I got up and waved to her.

"Iris!" she yelled delightedly. "Dori here's a clam. I can't get a thing out of her." *Dori.* Baby slapped the woman's shoulder over the fence. "Beautiful stranger!" She laughed so that her belly bulged through the chicken wire; then she coughed and drew on her cigarette. Stretched across her T-shirt were the words *Peak Performance.*

I smiled at the woman. She took one of the cigarettes that Baby held out to us, and for a while we stood and smoked in silence.

"You guys should come visit me sometime if you've nothing better to do," Baby said, and she turned to wink at Ilya, who was standing next to her mother. "I got a secret cat garden over there."

I saw Ilya's incredulous look and told her it was true.

"Thank you," the woman said politely. "We'd love to."

Baby ran a hand over her sweaty face and neck. "Come anytime. I'm generally in." She stubbed out her cigarette on the fence post and pushed the butt into her gold fanny pack. "I'll love you and leave you." She made to go, then turned back to me. "One thing, Iris. There's a man calling around town. Snooping."

I looked at the woman, who was staring impassively at Baby.

"I gave him what for, his head'll be throbbing for a long time." She laughed. "Just wanted to warn you."

Baby had almost vanished between the dry bushes that lined the wall to her property when, to my surprise, I heard the woman call her name. Baby stopped and turned.

"The man on the phone," the woman said. "What did he want?"

Baby shrugged. I saw her face light up with curiosity. At last she'd managed to lure the stranger out of her shell. The woman slipped through the gap in the fence and walked down the path through the dry grass toward Baby.

I hunkered down next to Ilya, glad that the conversation about the caller wasn't being held in her presence.

One of the cats was slinking low over the field a short distance from us, making for a point beyond Baby and the woman. "It's going to the cat garden," I said. "See it?"

Ilya nodded. We watched it slink slowly closer, then leap into the bushes behind Baby and vanish. "Want to see where it's gone?" I asked, and Ilya nodded again. She followed me through the gap in the fence and along the path. When we passed Baby and Ilya's mother, Baby was in full flow about her second husband.

The four of us spent the afternoon in Baby's shady walled garden. Time had stopped here. There was a lawn and a garden swing in the shade of two old apple trees. Few people knew that Baby had found a way of watering her garden—that she'd managed to preserve this little corner, almost as if nothing had changed.

She'd converted the shed into a cat sanctuary, where she offered them shelter, water, and dry food. Ilya and I sat on a towel on the grass, watching the cats come and go over the wall or through a flap in the door, watching them sleep in the shade and eat and drink.

I checked the wind direction every few minutes and kept an eye on the air-quality app. At about four, when the wind changed and the safety level switched from yellow to orange, I went into the house with Ilya. We sat on Baby's leather couch and zapped through the TV channels until we found a children's movie. I saw Baby and the woman smoking on the garden swing and wondered what they were talking about.

Again I thought of Ilya by the river, of the man on the phone, of the fact that the same man seemed to have called Baby. Ilya had moved close to me and was plucking absently at my T-shirt. A faint sadness came over me at the thought that there were no children in my life, or in Bad Heim, and that soon Ilya would be gone too. I wondered what she'd seen and heard at home—what she made of the fires and the goings-on here. For a moment I thought of asking her, but I didn't know how. She didn't speak much and was always shy around me. It seemed nosy to ask a lot of questions.

After supper I hung around in the dining room, hoping the woman would come out of her room again, as she sometimes did after putting Ilya to bed. I wanted to tell her about finding Ilya alone by the river. I waited a long time, but she didn't come that evening. Once I thought I heard something, but when I looked out the terrace door, the garden was empty in the warm night. All was still, even the forest. The sky over the hotel was a gray pall. I looked for the moon but couldn't find it.

It was almost three when I woke; I must have fallen asleep in front of the TV. All was dark and silent. I zapped through the programs; as so often, I ended up watching the local channel that reported on the situation in the forest. There was no news at this hour, but a number of heat-resistant webcams showed eerily green, mute images of the forest at night. I saw a grainy picture of the new camp, and above it, the activists' goals in big letters on a banner. A little way off, two emergency vehicles stood at the ready. The worst fires were now more or less under control again—but only for the time being. As long as it stayed hot—as long as it didn't rain—the fires would continue.

One of the tents was a bright, silent dome under the black sky; there must have been a light on inside. The activists slept in shifts, so there was always someone awake to defend the camp and wake the others if anything happened. I imagined them, the girl with the short hair and the other young people, their round shadows on the warm skin of the tent, alert, waiting.

Then, faint but strangely shrill, a noise burst through the silence of the camp, the silence of the dining room, the silence of the garden. A series of indistinct sounds. I went to the door and listened; it was coming from the garden. It repeated itself, broke off, then started up again.

Sometimes—rarely—injured animals dragged themselves here from the forest; the river must have fallen low enough in places for them to get across. I switched off

the TV and stared out into the darkness. A sense of unease gripped me—I remembered the fox in the garden
that I'd had to kill a few weeks back, its little black teeth,
its tail that was burned to the bone. I stepped cautiously
over the gravel. The noise grew louder, a wailing inter-
spersed with a strange gasping sound. At the door of
number five it was very close indeed. It wasn't coming
from the garden or from the forest. It was coming from
the room. When I knocked, it went quiet.

"Everything all right in there?"

No answer. I pushed down the handle; the door was
locked. I waited until the noise started up again, this
time accompanied by a scratching sound at the bottom
of the door. I went to fetch the spare key from reception, unlocked the door, and eased it open; when it was
an inch or two ajar something slipped through the gap
at my feet, scampered past me, and vanished through
the fence into the black field. It was the little gray cat.
It seemed unscathed; for a moment I saw its eyes in the
distance—two low, bright circles shining back at me.
Just a cat, soundless in the dark. I stood in the open
door, my heart thumping. The same sour smell I'd noticed a few days back hung in the room. I expected the
woman to come toward me through the darkness, and I
prepared a few words of explanation and apology—but
no one came. The room remained silent, as though its
occupants had gone, leaving only the cat, alone in the
stale sheets, stale smoke, perfume, hair spray.

I took a step into the room. The gentle sound of breathing came and went, barely audible; Ilya was lying in the middle of the big bed. But there was no one in the armchair at the window, no one behind the open door of the bathroom. The woman wasn't there. In the light of the outside lamp, Ilya's chest rose and fell under the sun on her pajama top. Rose and fell, rose and fell. She looked so small, her face so soft and still, her little fingers curled in loose fists on either side as if she were holding something very fragile.

I stood beside her, letting the warm night air fill the room. In the pockets of darkness around the bed, things began to take shape on the floor. I imagined cleaning the room, putting all the wrappers and old masks and empty plastic bottles in garbage bags, gathering up the towels and the still-warm sheets. I imagined going around with a damp rag, wiping up the little black marks that the woman left behind like a trail of breadcrumbs when she stubbed out her cigarettes. I imagined vacuuming, rubbing down the tiles and sink with vinegar, the mirror, the toilet seat. Pulling long, wet strands of blond hair out of the plughole. The sheets clean and white, pulled taut and tucked in at the corners. The windows open. The air, in this fantasy of mine, clear and fresh.

I don't know how long I stood there, between the child and the garden, unsure where things were headed. It wasn't until Ilya coughed that I noticed the burning smell. I closed the door from outside, leaving everything as I'd found it. The fire suddenly seemed very close—and there was Ilya, all alone in the last room in the row, the room backing onto the field that led to the forest. I stood on the veranda with the key, knowing I had to lock her in to conceal my intrusion and to make sure she didn't run away again. I imagined the woman faced with the same decision and wondered where she'd gone. From where I was standing I could see the forest, black at the end of the field. I could see the sky above it beginning to grow light. I walked quietly down the garden, past the fishpond and the maple, and through the gap in the fence. I went and stood under the window and waited with my back against the warm wall. Here and there a starling flew in the morning light; cats slunk through the grass. Somewhere behind the trees were the activists' tents; somewhere back there someone else was awake, keeping watch.

When at last a car drew up outside the hotel, I stayed where I was, listening. I heard the terrace door open and close, and bare feet tread gingerly over the wooden boards. I heard the key turn in the lock and the woman's quiet movements on the other side of the wall as she got into bed with the child. It was only now, as the tension fell away from me, that I realized how keyed up I'd been, terrified she wouldn't come back.

5

I woke late, still with the sense of unease I'd felt in the night. I got up and showered. No one was around as I made my way to the kitchen. I was glad Ilya wasn't playing in the garden yet—glad to be alone with my thoughts for a while longer. I put coffee on to brew and went to reception. There, lying on the desk, were my car keys. I hadn't taken the car out since the day I'd seen the woman and Ilya on the highway, and afterward I'd put the keys back in the drawer under the counter, as I always did. Until now, I'd assumed the woman had come back in a taxi that morning. I walked out the front door to the parking lot. My Golf was there. I couldn't see anything out of the ordinary. There were face masks on the passenger seat, chewing-gum wrappers, a lighter. I got in and sat down. Nothing had been adjusted: seat, mirrors, everything as ever. Only the windshield looked as if it might have been recently washed; gray streaks in the film of ash charted the movement of the wipers. There were also hand marks on the metal and on the windows, but they could just as well have been mine. I was about to lock the car again when I spotted something on the floor in front of the driver's seat. Among the footprints in the dust and ash was the thin gold chain I'd once noticed on the woman's wrist. A single charm hung from it—a tiny star.

Back in the hotel I locked the car keys in the small safe that I kept in a cabinet at reception. Inside were travel documents forgotten by a guest years ago, a few pieces of jewelry that had belonged to my mother, and some cash. I didn't want the woman driving off at night again, and locking the keys away seemed like the easiest way to stop her.

I put the charm bracelet in the pocket of my dress. I thought it might be an opening to a conversation, a chance to find out why the woman had borrowed my car and where she'd gone in it. More than once I prepared things to say and then rejected them. I didn't want to upset her; I was afraid she'd take offense and maybe even leave.

It was quiet all day. I drank iced tea, read, sunbathed. I didn't see Ilya or the woman, but I heard the TV in their room and imagined them sitting on the bed in their pajamas, drinking lemonade and eating little cakes wrapped in cellophane, the woman the worse for wear after her sleepless night, unkempt and unmade-up, drawing occasionally on a cigarette, Ilya spellbound by the stories on the screen, plucking at her mother's top the way she'd plucked at mine the day before. Sometimes I heard them laugh.

In the afternoon, when the garden was in the shade, they came out. Ilya was carrying a Barbie and a little see-through bag. She came over to me and set out a row of tiny clothes, cowboy boots, and hairbrushes on my lounger. It was the first time she'd approached me of her own accord. I admired the things she showed me and thought of the dolls and doll clothes that were somewhere in my apartment, and the bright-pink house that folded into a suitcase. The woman sat down next to us, and I offered her something to drink and fetched more glasses, ice, and lemons from the kitchen. We exchanged a few words about the weather, the continuing heat, the situation in the forest. Then I took out the chain.

"Is this yours?" My voice sounded unnaturally high.

She grasped her left wrist. "I hadn't even noticed I'd lost it." I dropped the chain into her outstretched hand. "Thank you! Where was it?"

"In the parking lot," I lied. "Next to my car."

The woman frowned. "Really? That's strange," she said, and then smiled, as though amused that the chain should lead a life of its own.

I was amazed that she could keep her composure to such an extent, not losing control of her face for a second. There was nothing in her eyes or smile to suggest she felt caught out or uncomfortable—only genuine-seeming surprise. It was hard to believe she'd been out in my car and left Ilya on her own. If I hadn't found her bracelet in the footwell, I'd have thought I was imagining things.

I asked where she'd gotten the chain. "It's very pretty," I said.

"Do you think so?" She looked at the thin coil of gold in her hand, the glinting charm. "Ilya's father gave it to me. When Ilya was born."

"Then it must be very precious to you."

She was silent, her eyes on Ilya, absorbed in her game.

"Will he be joining you here?" I asked, and again my voice sounded strangely high. I felt nosy and immediately regretted the question, but the woman smiled and said nothing, her face quite smooth.

"Do *you* want children?" she asked after a pause, her eyes on Ilya again. When I didn't immediately reply she apologized. "I only ask because of the bracelet. Not everyone's cut out for it."

I wondered if she was talking about me or herself. I thought back to the night—of Ilya sleeping peacefully, alone in the hotel room with the little cat; of my mother and Grandad and the rows I'd heard through the wall when they thought I was asleep. His words, *You're no kind of mother for the child.* Her silence. I saw myself in Auntie's bed, under the bright square of light that shone through the curtain onto my coverlet from the outside lamp. My hand, pale gray in the light, as if cut off from the rest of my body. Was Mom not my mother? My hand in the dark. Was there another mother somewhere, with black hair and long fingers like me—a mother who lived somewhere else, with a father and other children? I imagined the life of this unknown mother and her family, every day the same; I saw a bird's-eye view of four plates on a tablecloth. My hand—light, dark, light, dark until I fell asleep. Mom creeping into bed with me in the middle of the night.

When I set off to do some shopping later that afternoon I ran into the woman and Ilya outside the hotel. The woman was wearing a mask and sunglasses again; a pale-blue silk scarf covered her hair. Ilya, also in a mask, was standing next to her. They were going into town too. We walked along the sidewalk together, the woman pushing the empty stroller. The asphalt still held the day's heat, and the air hung heavy between the houses and over the parched front gardens.

"You said you had pictures of the old days?" She spoke diffidently, raising a hand from the stroller and waving her own question aside as if she didn't like asking favors. When I suggested we look through the boxes together that evening she jumped at the offer. We'd be alone together, I thought. Maybe I'd be able to find out more about her and her situation. I decided I'd offer her my help—ask her to let me know when she had to go out so that I could keep an eye on Ilya.

We walked side by side in silence until we came to the stores. I had various things to pick up or order, and stopped off at the dry cleaner's, the pharmacy, the drugstore. The woman and child came with me, greeting people politely whenever I stopped to chat. The topics were always the same. The heat, the forest, what the warning app said, which towns had been evacuated. The greengrocer complained that she couldn't get local produce anymore. No apples and pears, no plums, no cherries; nothing grew these days. She asked the woman what brought her here, to this dying region—and with a child too. But she got no answer.

The only store the woman seemed interested in for herself was the pharmacy. She bought painkillers and asked for various antihistamines. She knew exactly what she wanted, cited names and dosages. Doxylamine, promethazine, hydroxyzine. The pharmacist advised her at length, but she seemed barely to hear. She nodded and smiled politely, and I had the impression it wasn't the first time she'd listened to monologues of this kind. She paid for the drugs that were available over the counter, put her mask back on, and said goodbye.

Outside she asked if I'd like to put my parcel of dry cleaning on the bottom of the stroller. As she hung the bag from the pharmacy over one of the handles, she explained, without being asked, that she suffered from headaches and insomnia. I nodded. I thought of her nighttime getaway, of Ilya alone in the room. Ilya was in the stroller now and looked ready to fall asleep. I noticed she was no longer wearing her mask.

Slowly we headed back toward the hotel. I glanced at the app and saw a dark-red zone moving across the map from forest to town. The more I thought about the child's lack of protection, the more alarmed I felt. I hesitated, wondering if I should say something. "The air's getting worse," I said eventually. "I think Ilya's taken her mask off."

"Oh!" The woman stopped and leaned over the canopy. "You must think I'm a dreadful mother." She began to rummage frantically through the bottom of the stroller, her purse, the bag from the pharmacy.

In the end I found the mask under my parcel of dry cleaning, but by then the woman was a nervous wreck, looking repeatedly in the same places and dashing around the stroller, apologizing to me and Ilya in turn. When at last we went on our way and the child had fallen asleep, she thanked me, laying her hand on my bare arm. Her fingers were quite cold.

The sky was tipping over into a colorless evening, but the heat persisted. Above us, three small planes headed for the forest. We stopped to watch them. "Crop dusters," the woman said. "Is that a firefighting squadron?"

I didn't know.

"I think it might be." She moved her head back and forth, as though it were only the poor visibility that prevented her from identifying the planes and their purpose. They grew smaller and quieter and eventually disappeared altogether. We went slowly on our way.

"They were old planes," she said. "The rescue squadron probably has more modern ones." I asked her how she knew so much. To my astonishment, she told me she used to have a pilot's license. "Not for a long time, though," she said. "I stopped renewing it years ago."

I looked at her hands pushing the stroller, her short nails, her firm grip. I remembered the coldness of her touch. There was something determined about those hands, a physical strength at odds with her nervousness, her apparent reluctance to take up space.

"I was a different person before I married," she said, and I wasn't sure if she was talking to me or herself. "Do you ever have the feeling there was a point in your life when you took the wrong turn? That the whole rest of your life depends on that one moment?"

I pondered this. "There was someone once," I said. "But it wouldn't have worked out forever."

I shrugged. We looked at each other over our masks. Again, I noticed the unusual color of her eyes.

"She moved away," I said. "She's with another woman and has a child Ilya's age."

I thought of Paula, as I almost always did—of her hair, her hands. At some point my memory of her had grown rigid, reduced to those single static details. I'd forgotten the smell of her, the feel of her body.

"Are you still in touch?"

I nodded. "We call each other sometimes. She worries about the fires. Her mother still lives here."

My memories mingled with possible versions of a present, paths not taken. My life, Bad Heim, the hotel. Paula hadn't understood why I clung to everything here.

"Is there a point like that in *your* life?" I asked the woman. She said nothing, her eyes fixed on the empty road ahead. Then she turned to me for a moment as if she were smiling, but I couldn't see her mouth because of the mask. The sidewalk we were on led straight to the hotel. Ilya was asleep in the stroller. We walked slowly through the quiet, oppressive evening.

"What will you do when you have to move away?" the woman asked at length, leaving my question unanswered. "When the region's no longer inhabitable, I mean."

She said *when*, not *if*, as though it were inevitable—as though she were speaking of a near future, two or three or five years from now. It sounded like the diagnosis of a disease whose precise course was unclear, but whose end was certain. I looked at the pale sky reflected in the hotel windows, the old-fashioned sign over the door.

"I hope it won't come to that."

"Oh," she said, turning to me again. "Yes, of course." There was pity in her voice. We both knew how naïve my hope was.

6

Later, when she'd put Ilya to bed, the woman came out into the garden, where I was sitting reading on one of the loungers. A wall of smoke was rising over the forest.

She asked if she could join me; she was holding a slim book in her hand. "I've been reading about Bad Heim," she told me, turning it so that I could see the title. *Circling*, it said, stamped in silver on green cloth. *Poems*. The author's name, Ada Lumin, meant nothing to me. For a while we sat side by side, reading our books—then I noticed that the woman was holding hers open on her lap and staring at the forest. When she saw me looking at her she said, "Hard to imagine it's the same place." She held up the book. "Would you like to hear the description of Bad Heim?" I hesitated, and she added, "I could read it to you if you like." Then, as if this required explanation: "I'm actually an actor."

Her voice sounded different when she read. There was a softness to the words, an innocence I wouldn't have expected of her—then her voice seemed to roughen and break. It was harsh when the text allowed for it, with rapid syllables and gaps—even gulfs—between the words. Then it softened again and the lines flowed. I stared through the warm darkness toward the forest, listening to her voice describing Bad Heim as it had once been: tranquil and beautiful, set in lush countryside—a garden, a sigh of relief. I almost had the impression the poem had been written exactly where we were sitting, with the same view toward the edge of the forest, the same knowledge of the cool river dividing the trees.

It was a long poem. I was surprised how easy I found it to listen to the woman, how moved I was by her reading. I looked at her, at her face in the glow of the lamp, the furrow between her brows. The last line was repeated.

I would stay. But that's too little.
I would stay. But that's too little.

Afterward we sat in silence. I heard her breathing. I heard her close the book.

"Forgive me. I hope it wasn't too long for you." There was insecurity in her eyes. She asked me again to forgive her. "I enjoyed it. But I shouldn't have forced myself on you."

"Thank you," I said quickly, laying my hand on her arm. "I thought it was very beautiful." I couldn't quite find words for what her reading had made me feel. Something twitched in her eyebrow, at the corner of her mouth, as if she wasn't sure she believed me. "You're very good at it."

She smiled and held my gaze. I thought I saw a hint of triumph, or the memory of it. Then she turned away, brushed it aside. "It's a long time since I was any good at it."

I took her into my private apartment to look for the photographs. After my grandfather's death I'd cleared his things into the guest room, where all the family relics were kept. The other room, my bedroom, was practically empty. There was a bed under the window, a bookcase, and an old chest of drawers for my clothes. A small painting of a bunch of marguerites hung over the bed in a thin black frame. It had been painted by my grandmother and was discreetly signed with her initials in the bottom-right-hand corner. It was the only thing from Bad Heim that my mother had always taken with her, always hung up. However often we moved, however many new rooms we had, that picture always had a place. When I cleared my grandfather's things into the guest room—and with them the things he'd inherited from his parents and from his wife and daughter—I had found my mother's little suitcase at the back of his closet. Inside, right at the top, was the picture, lying with her hairbrush on an unwashed pale-blue sweater. Everything still bore her mark, all those years on. There was a tangle of hair in the brush and a spatter of brown stains—maybe coffee she'd spilled—on the sweater collar. The things still smelled of her. Grandad must have been given them in the hospital when she died and never managed to unpack them.

I stood next to the woman in the light of a bare bulb, facing a wall of cardboard boxes, crates, and suitcases. On the other side of the room, dresses, suits, and coats jostled against the glass panes of an old-fashioned closet, and rows of shelves were stacked with boxes of china wrapped in yellow tissue paper, sewing machines, cookbooks, shaving brushes, spectacles, roller skates. Cross-country skis and poles stood in a corner.

All the boxes were labeled, and I worked my way from one label to the next. I found my Barbie dolls and got out the Barbie suitcase house for Ilya. The woman stood at a bookcase lined with various tomes and picture books, preserving jars, hatboxes, old purses, table-tennis paddles. Farther along she ran her hand over a dusty blond wig. "Who did all these things belong to?" Behind her the closet was bursting with lace and silk and cotton, floral prints, spotted prints, felt, and woolens—and the white fur that my mother had loved so much.

Meanwhile I'd found the box of photo albums. Slim cardboard folders marked with the year. Sleeved pages where my grandfather had arranged the pictures chronologically. Nothing had been weeded out, nothing was labeled.

When I turned to the woman she was holding a short dress up to her body and looking at herself in the glass of the closet doors. It had been one of my mother's party dresses, a shiny black strapless affair with flounces at the hem. Seeing the woman with it brought back memories of my mother hugging me goodbye—the smell of her perfume, the chill of her big earrings on my neck.

"Don't you ever wear it, Iris?" she asked, and then immediately corrected herself. "Ms. Lehmann."

I laughed. "You can call me Iris."

She turned to me. I remembered that her name was Dorota; now she introduced herself as Dori. She looked at me and I caught another glimpse of her little tooth. "It would suit you, Iris." She held out the dress to me.

"But what would I do in it?" I asked, laughing again. "Clean the rooms? Do the groceries?" Her gaze unnerved me; I wanted to duck away from it. I wasn't used to being looked at like that. She rocked her head back and forth, still smiling.

"Occasions can be created."

I saw myself next to her, reflected in the glass, the box of albums between us. My upper body, my neck, my distorted face. I saw her reflection lower the dress and slowly fold it, running her fingers over the hem.

We carried the pictures and doll things into the dining room, and I went to fetch something to drink. When I got back, Dori was already bent over the open albums, studying each picture in turn—photos of local people, guests, and friends, most of them taken in color with a simple handheld camera. I'd been afraid it would upset me to look at them—afraid the past would prove painful—but the albums were from a time when only a small part of my life had taken place in Bad Heim; it wasn't until later, when my mother died, that the world in these photos had become mine. I recognized my aunt, who looked very much as I remembered her—a woman who never followed a fashion. I spotted Baby. Grandad. The old garden. People from Bad Heim, some of them still alive. People who still came to see me sometimes. People who'd grown old. There was only one picture of me. It was taken in the dining room, which I didn't immediately recognize, though the décor hadn't changed since then. I was sitting at a crowded table in a frilly white dress, a big shiny white bow in my black hair. On the tablecloth, next to the brass ashtray that was still there today, was my mother's hand. I knew it immediately—her long fingers and round fuchsia nails, the little ring with the green stone that was now in the safe at reception.

"Is that you?" Dori peered at the photo. "Was it your first communion?"

I couldn't remember the day the photo was taken—only the dress. I remembered my mother buying it for me in Munich, together with a pair of red leather sandals. I shook my head. "My mother just liked dressing me up."

I was glad you could see only her hand in the picture, not her face. She'd never belonged in Bad Heim. There was one photo of her I really loved. I didn't know who'd taken it, but it made her look as if she were holding a rifle, as if nothing could get in her way. I kept it in a box in my room, together with some letters and her diaries, but I never looked inside. I was too afraid of reviving memories of her face, her voice.

"You grew up here?"..."Did you know your father?"..."Is your mother still alive?"

I had the feeling that Dori was comparing her life with the things I told her, comparing my childhood with the decisions she faced concerning herself and Ilya. My reminiscences seemed to make her happy. The road trips, the nights spent on friends' couches or at parties or in the car. The songs my mother had made up for me, the stories she'd added to every day for weeks or months—our own little world.

Dori and I sat for a long time at the big table in the now-quiet dining room. We puzzled over the unknown faces, wondering if one of them might be Ada Lumin's. After a while I stopped looking at the pictures; I sat and smoked, pouring wine, answering Dori's questions, reminiscing. I often didn't know myself what was being celebrated—whose wedding or retirement party we were looking at. Dori studied every picture.

"Is that why you're here?" I asked. "Because of the poems?"

Her short tooth flashed in the lamplight. Her cheeks were flushed, and there was a dull gleam in her eyes. She moved her head somewhere between yes and no. "In the poem I read you, Bad Heim sounded so appealing. A place of calm. I had no idea about the fires." She paused, figuring out what to say next. "It's not just the place that's important either. I had the feeling that the woman who wrote the poems...a lot of it resonated with me." She shrugged and laughed as if it didn't matter. "It was naïve of me not to find out more."

I nodded. Nothing that had been written about the area thirty years ago held true today.

"The hotel's the same," I said. "The hotel never changes." I said it lightly, with a laugh, and realized, even as I spoke, that it wasn't true. The photos had made that all too clear. The hotel had been a place where people vacationed and celebrated, a place of community, a family hotel. None of that existed now.

We were silent for a moment. I would have liked to ask Dori more—about the book, her marriage, the place she'd left behind. But this felt like a good point to bring the conversation round to Ilya. I cleared my throat.

"You know how you went out yesterday morning?"

She nodded.

"Ilya must have walked out of the hotel while you were gone." I saw in her face that she didn't grasp what I was saying. "I found her alone in the forest, by the river."

Slowly my words seemed to filter through to her. She sat in silence over the open album on the table. It was hard to tell what was going on in her head. Her face was tense and pale; there was a mixture of doubt and fear in her eyes. I felt I should defuse the situation, bring back the levity between us, but I didn't know how.

"She said something about being in the forest with you, but I thought she'd made it up."

"I worry about the fires," I said, as if she weren't aware of the danger. "You can always leave her with me if that would help. I like being with her."

Dori nodded and lit a cigarette. "Thank you for bringing her back." She blew out smoke. "I'm sorry we're causing you all this trouble. I just don't know where else to go right now."

"I'm glad to have you here," I said, and realized it was true. I liked having life in the hotel again, having a child around. I liked having Dori around.

"There are a couple of things I'm trying to figure out," she said into the smoke. "I lie awake at night and can't think straight and then I panic, lying there in that silent room. It feels like everything around me is collapsing."

I nodded. I thought of the caller who was looking for her, Alexander Vargas. The packs of pills she'd bought in the pharmacy. I imagined her driving my car, the oncoming headlights passing over her face—then realized I was mixing imagination and memory, realized it was my mother's face I was seeing, the face I'd seen on so many aimless drives, so many freeways and highways.

Dori began to defend herself. "I thought she was asleep. I'd never have dreamed she'd walk that far on her own."

Not knowing what else to do, I topped up her glass. I thought of the caller again and of what Baby had said about Dori being on the run. She didn't know where to go, I thought—what strange times these were. I laid my hand on hers.

"Don't worry, she's safe."

We drank and smoked. I tried to remember when I'd last sat with someone like this.

"I can't imagine what it means to be responsible for a child," I said, but she didn't reply, apparently deep in thought. When I repeated my offer to take care of Ilya, she smiled and thanked me absently. I decided to change the subject and asked about her acting work—were there any movies I might have seen her in?

She shook her head. "I was mainly in theater."

I stole a glance at her face. She didn't dominate the room as my mother's theater friends had done—but her voice! I could still hear her reading, not a hint of her usual smooth control.

"I stopped when I was pregnant with Ilya," she said.

"It must have been hard to combine an acting career with motherhood," I said. "All those rehearsals and performances."

She shook her head. "That wasn't so much the problem. I just couldn't act anymore. I couldn't do it." She lit another cigarette. I imagined her on stage, speaking someone else's words, her heavily made-up face in the bright light. Before today I couldn't have imagined it. I remembered what she'd said on our walk about being a different person before she got married.

"I thought it would come back; I thought, give it a few weeks or months and it would come back. But it didn't. My craft, the thing I was good at—it was gone." She opened her palms a little, as if it were vanishing then and there. As if to show they were empty. "The emotions, the empathy. The ability to get inside another person, to feel their love, their despair." She paused and looked down at her firm white fingers, lying open on the photos of old Bad Heim.

"My husband got what he wanted," she went on. "I haven't done any acting for four years, and now it's too late to get back into it. I've lost the knack." She sipped her wine. "That's what Ada Lumin's poems are about. The sense of losing yourself." She fell silent again and blew thin clouds of smoke into the space between us. "I don't feel anything anymore. And yet, to love someone the way you love a child...I'd often played mothers, but this feeling you have when you become a parent, this fear—it's like everything's suddenly a matter of life and death, every decision could potentially harm your child. They could fall or get sick or injure themselves or die. They could turn out like me or like him. It kills you just thinking about it." The ends of her words were swallowed up as she sucked on her cigarette. Half words drifted over the table with the smoke, hung in the air.

"I'd lost this thing I'd always been good at. Until then I'd been able to immerse myself completely in a role, another life. Even as a child. I could be whoever I wanted." Suddenly she raised her arms, palms up, as if to say *There you have it, ladies and gentlemen!* A brilliant smile spread across her face, so genuine that I was almost startled when she switched it off again. It was the smile of an actor whose part she'd played for a couple of seconds—maybe the actor she had once been herself. It was a smile that no longer hid her tooth, a smile that banished all tension from her face. The transformation came as a strange surprise and seemed to hold the key to her contradictions.

Dori caught my eye before I could look away. She'd seen—she must have—the effect she'd had on me. A slight twitch at the corner of her mouth, a faint smile. She touched my arm with her hand. Then she said, "I can't do it anymore. I live only for Ilya. Only as a mother for Ilya."

The albums were closed now, and Dori's hands lay limply on top, the thin gold chain from her husband around her wrist. Next to it I could see the year in Grandad's small, old-fashioned handwriting. My mother had died two years later. Grandad's words came back to me. *You're no kind of mother for the child.*

"It's no big deal." Dori sat up and smoothed her hair. "It was always just a game. You don't save lives acting."

She'd reverted to the person she'd been when she arrived. I sat helpless in front of this façade, not knowing what to say. "I have Ilya now," she added with a smile, as if that were enough. "I don't feel comfortable acting anymore."

Soon afterward, she left to go to bed, but she came back while I was clearing the table. She stood in the open door. "Could you keep it to yourself that you found Ilya in the forest? That I wasn't around?"

I said no one would ask anyway—and thought of Alexander Vargas. She looked at me as if I didn't get it. "I mean when you talk to Ilya. If you don't mind, I think it would be best not to mention it to her. Style it out if she asks. Make a game of it, tell her you don't remember. It would be best if she thought the whole thing never happened."

I nodded slowly. Dori stood there, fixing me with her eyes. "You won't say anything to her?" She waited in the door until I'd said the words—until I'd promised not to talk to her daughter about the incident in the forest.

Then she, too, nodded, relieved. "Good. Great. Thank you so much."

I saw her through the black glass walking slowly back along the veranda. I saw her stop outside her door and turn to look at the forest. I thought of her face. Her insistence that I promise to keep quiet struck me as out of character, and it was a while before I figured out the reason. There was something she was afraid of. Something she was more afraid of than the fires and the bad air.

7

The third time the man called, the TV was announcing a new heat record for the day. Fresh smoke was billowing over the forest, and the police had been broadcasting warnings again since early morning. *Stay home, wear face masks, keep doors and windows shut.* Children and the elderly were advised to take a bath every three hours—the water not too cold, around ninety-three degrees. I'd filled an old zinc tub for Ilya in the kitchen. Between baths we sat in the gray light of the curtained dining room.

"Is this a good time to call?" the man asked. I stood behind the counter at reception looking across at his wife and daughter. Ilya was bent over an old coloring book; Dori was sitting next to her, reading.

"What can I do for you?"

"I've had confirmation that my wife and daughter are in Bad Heim."

I said nothing. The wind blew gusts of warm air against the windows.

"Has anyone been in touch with you?"

No, I said, no one had been in touch.

"My wife bought something in Bad Heim yesterday, in a pharmacy."

It felt like a trap. He was probably planning to come and fetch them.

"I already told you," I said slowly. "I can't give you a room."

"That's not why I'm calling. I wanted to ask for your help." When I didn't reply he added, "I would, of course, pay you for your trouble."

"I don't understand."

"It's complicated. I can't go into the details, but my wife isn't in a position to care for the child. She needs help, professional help." He sounded very calm, but it was a controlled calm, as if he had little choice.

"Why don't you come here yourself?" I asked.

He hesitated, as though searching for the right words. "My wife doesn't trust me. She...I wanted to help her, but she doesn't trust me. She thinks I want to make her take meds, she thinks I want to take the child away from her. If I came to pick her up...I'm afraid it would only make things worse. Do you understand? She has to come back of her own free will, she has to accept that she needs help."

Dori and Ilya were talking quietly in the dining room. I turned up the TV.

"I just want my daughter to be safe. Do you understand? Bad Heim is no place for a child. You know yourself how things are there."

I said nothing. He was right, of course; I knew very well that Bad Heim in summer was no longer a place to vacation. And yet his words hurt. I felt them as an attack—on life in Bad Heim, on Ilya's little existence here.

"My wife's sick," the man went on. "She can't take care of a child. I'm extremely concerned."

"What do you mean?"

"It's complicated. She's unstable. She doesn't know danger when she sees it. It's very important that someone keep an eye on her, you understand. That things don't get out of control. If I get the police involved, she'll freak out. And I don't want to put my daughter through that, do you understand? I need someone on the ground, someone discreet. I don't want the situation to escalate."

I asked again what he meant.

"I don't know. I can't see inside her head. I don't know what state she's in. I fear the worst."

I noticed that my memories were prejudicing me against the man—that my reactions were determined not by him or Dori but by what I'd seen and heard as a child. I was reminded of Grandad, convinced Mom wasn't capable of looking after me, treating her like a child until the day he died. Of course, I knew nothing of these people's marriage, but something in the man's tone was unpleasantly familiar to me. His arrogance, his assumption that he had a better grasp of his wife's life and health than she did. His attempt to color my image of Dori, although I was a complete stranger to him. It felt wrong. It felt like manipulation. Hoping to get rid of him, I promised to keep my eyes peeled. It seemed to be the opening he'd been waiting for.

"Would you mind asking around a bit? Maybe in the pharmacy. Can you find out where she's staying? I tried making inquiries myself, but you know how it is for an outsider."

I thought of Baby, who kept a whistle handy to blow down the phone if she didn't like the sound of the caller.

"As I said, I will of course reimburse you for your trouble," he went on, as if I'd already agreed. "Things can't be easy for you financially."

I made no comment, only confirming that I would keep a lookout.

"Do you still have my number?"

I said I did, but he dictated it to me again anyway. I knew he'd call again—and keep on and on calling until Dori went back to him.

After we'd hung up, I stood at reception for a while longer, looking across at Dori and Ilya. Dori had put her book aside and been cajoled into coloring—a child's face, an arm, a shoe. Red cheeks, purple eyelids. *I fear the worst*, the man had said. *I fear the worst.*

The more time passed on this hot, windowless day, the more acutely I felt the uncertainty that the call had unleashed in me. I watched to see if Dori stuck to the three-hour intervals. I checked the temperature of the bathwater, kept an eye on how much Ilya drank, put out a bowl of canned mandarins and pineapple for them. Several times I thought I spotted neglect—Dori absent, absorbed in her book as the minute hand ticked past the hour. But she always remembered in the end; I never had to remind her. She sat next to the tub with her feet in the water while Ilya bathed. She pushed around the old plastic boats I'd found in a box. She patted Ilya dry with a towel, helped her into her panties and thin summer dress. It irritated me that my conversation with the man had forced me into a responsibility I found intrusive and ultimately unnecessary, and I decided to speak to Dori.

Late that evening I knocked softly at the door of number five.

Dori opened up. "What is it?" she whispered. I saw Ilya asleep on the bed behind her. As there was still a ban on being outside, she asked me in. We closed the door against the smoke, and Dori laid a rolled-up towel along the gap at the bottom as I'd shown her. Then we stood facing each other in the dark. I took off my mask.

"Hang on a sec." I heard her in the darkness, saw her gray figure grope its way along the wall. She switched on the bathroom light and beckoned to me. "Do you mind coming in here?" she asked. "I don't want to wake Ilya. It took her so long to get to sleep tonight."

The bathroom was strewn with various medicines, drops and oils, powder compacts, lipsticks, a hair dryer, a hairbrush, bottles of different-colored nail polish. Dori began to tidy up. She screwed lids on jars and bottles and lined everything up in a row.

"Your husband called today," I said, and saw her face, impassive in the mirror. She was trying to clean the sink with her fingers, rubbing dry stains, scratching with her nails, rinsing old suds, powder residue, and hair down the drain. "He's looking for you and Ilya."

"What did you tell him?"

"That no one's allowed to stay here at the moment. That I can't help him."

She looked at me in the mirror.

"I didn't know how much I could say."

I heard myself speak these words as if they were scripted—words from a book or movie, a story someone had made up. Dori continued to look at me; a spasm of emotion crossed her face and she laughed the toneless laugh that had become familiar to me.

"Did he frighten you?"

I didn't reply. It sounded as though she were asking if he'd threatened me, but that hadn't been the problem. Alexander Vargas was calm and polite—and yet every time the phone rang I was terrified it would be him.

"Did he tell you I'm sick and can't look after my child?"

Her face had taken on a hard expression. She turned the faucet off and then on again, washed her hands, sat down on the edge of the tub. Her wet fingers gripped her skirt, leaving dark patches on the blue cloth. I stood tall in front of her, looking down—at her straight white part, her clenched wet hands.

"Is he coming here? Is he?"

She stood up and began to toss the things she'd lined up into a little bag.

"All he knows is that you bought something in town. He doesn't know you're in the hotel."

She closed her eyes. "The pharmacy." She was breathing fast. She sat down again, got up again. "Do you know if the trains are running? Do you have your phone on you?"

The small room suddenly felt cramped. Dori squeezed past me into the bedroom. The bathroom light fell through the door onto the floor, the bed. I saw Dori's back. I watched her bustle around gathering things up, carrying armfuls of stuff to the chair, setting some things aside, fetching others.

"He won't come," I whispered. "He said he doesn't want the situation to escalate."

She didn't look at me but went on piling things haphazardly onto the armchair. "He wants to take her away from me. When he finds us, he'll take her away." She spun around and came back to me. "Did you tell him about finding Ilya in the forest? Did you tell him she was there on her own? Without me?"

I quickly shook my head. "Why are you so scared? No one can take your child from you just like that."

Not a word. She looked at me; her face twitched again. She turned away and went on with her preparations, pulling the suitcase from under the bed. "Can you drive us to the station? Or call us a taxi?"

"He says he just wants to know how you are. He says he's worried."

Again that toneless laugh. "Do you believe him? Do you agree that I can't look after my child?"

"I don't know what to think."

I stood in the door. I saw my shadow. I saw her gray feet, her restless hands.

After a while I said, "Where are you thinking of going? I don't think he'll come here. He asked me to keep an eye on you and Ilya. We can figure something out, figure out what I tell him and what not."

I recognized the voice I was using; I remembered how it felt to talk in this way. *Nice and easy now, nice and easy.* How it felt to hold someone who was close to the edge. I thought of my mother, of the evenings and nights spent at her bedside, wondering what I could do to help her, how I could make things better. Childlike ideas running through my head until at last everything softened, her hand in mine, her arms, her face on the pillow.

There, there.

"You can tell me what I should tell him and what not," I repeated.

I could feel Dori growing calmer. The initial fright, the impulse to flee, was beginning to wear off.

"We can figure something out," I said again. "Make a plan."

There, there.

She looked at me.

I nodded at her until she nodded back. Until she put down whatever was in her hand and came into the bathroom. She sat back down on the side of the tub.

"Did he offer to pay you?" she asked, and when I nodded she laughed. "Of course he did."

We were silent. She fetched her cigarettes from her purse, inhaled deeply, blew slow clouds of smoke into the tiny room. What could we do?

"It took me a long time to figure out what he does. He calls me crazy so often that I start to believe it myself. He tells me I've forgotten something, or that something didn't happen, and in the end I don't know what's true."

She looked at me through the smoke in the yellow light of the old bathroom lamp and came suddenly closer—a little too close. "See this?" She opened her mouth and pointed to her front teeth, then turned to the mirror and ran a finger over the little dip. Her voice had grown louder, but now, with a glance at the door, she went back to whispering. "I threw myself down the stairs. I couldn't bear it anymore. I know it sounds like I'm the crazy one, but he's the one who makes me that way. I didn't know how else to get away from him. He just keeps on and on and on and on. There's no end to it. Wait here." She went out again and came back with her phone.

"I've had it switched off for days. It was too much for me. If I switch it on there'll be hundreds of messages from him."

I didn't think there was anything weird about that. He was looking for her, after all, and she'd gone off with their child; under the circumstances it seemed only natural that the man should try to get hold of his wife. But what she showed me when she switched on the phone was more than I'd expected. A salvo of messages appeared on her screen: *Alexander, Alexander, Alexander.* There was no end to it. She opened her chat app. He'd sent mainly voice messages. Several-minute-long voice messages: 255 and counting, according to the app. 280…283. The man had sent 283 voice messages in six days. Hours of messages. She clicked on one at random. It was a calm male voice that I immediately recognized. The same pitch, the same slight drawl—only the politeness he'd shown toward me was absent. I wondered what it must do to her to endure such treatment—the coldness, the scorn. We were both standing now, smoking, the phone quivering between us, a little blue dot moving across the screen as the man spoke. Dori opened another message, and another, and yet another. He spoke about himself and about her, dredging up old stories, listing things she'd done wrong, things she'd failed to do, things she couldn't afford to do. He named one shortcoming after another; her lack of character, her weakness, and—over and over—the trauma, the endless, overwhelming suffering she'd put their daughter through, the unforgivable consequences of her actions. She'd already damaged the child psychologically; if she carried on the way she was going, she'd soon have a small dead body on her hands.

Dori's face was impassive. She listened to his words as if she were made of stone. Only once, when he suddenly raised his voice, she jumped and started toward the door to check on Ilya—to make sure she was still asleep and couldn't hear anything.

"Can we turn it off?" I asked. I couldn't take any more.

"I'm sorry," she said. "I'm used to it." She'd stubbed out her cigarette in the sink, leaving a black speck that slowly blurred on the wet porcelain. She sat back down on the edge of the tub. I looked around and perched opposite her on the toilet lid.

"Is he doing this because you've left him? Is it new?"

Dori shook her head. "I can't remember when it started. At some point—this was before Ilya—I noticed that I'd started lying to him. I was afraid of what he might make of things, afraid he'd see things I didn't see. I didn't want him twisting everything till I was choking with guilt." She searched for a memory, an example. "Once I forgot something when I did the groceries, something he'd wanted and had specially asked for.

Canned peaches. I didn't remember until I was almost home, and by then the store was closed. So I put on a little act. Chucked everything—the lot. When I got home I told him I'd gotten dizzy on the way there and had to turn back." She laughed, as if it were someone else's story, the story of a woman she had no sympathy with. "Sickness was always my go-to. Sickness and pain, that's something he respects. He's a doctor."

An image hovered between us: her groceries in the black of a garbage can, her hands burying them under the trash so he wouldn't find them.

"In the book I read to you from, *Circling*, there's this line, 'He eats me up till nothing's left.' That's how it felt. After a while it all seemed normal to me. Always having to probe his mood, predict his reaction, explain myself, make excuses. Always terrified of slipping up, of forgetting something again. Then we had Ilya and it got even worse. *You're turning our daughter into a junkie*—because she still had a pacifier at eighteen months. Most children have a pacifier at that age, but for him it was a sign that I was lazy and selfish." She stared at the brown wall tiles, the old-fashioned light switch next to the door.

I studied her profile—the straight nose, the soft mouth.

"I know I shouldn't have taken her away from him. He's not a bad person or a bad father." She looked at me. "He means well, I really think he does. I should have taken a firmer stance years ago—I don't know why I got so scared. He never laid a hand on me, there was no genuine violence. I should have talked with him, should have behaved differently toward him, but instead I turned into this woman who apologizes for everything, lies all the time, keeps her head down, nods and says sorry and can't do anything without being scared of what he'll say. At some point I realized I was acting like a child of Ilya's age. Like he was my father as well as hers—except that he's soft on her and hard on me."

I laid my hand on hers, still holding the phone. Her fingers were cold.

"What he does is violence," I said. We sat facing one another for a moment.

Then she made a gesture as if it wasn't worth talking about, as if she'd already said too much. "There's always a dynamic to these things. We bring out the worst in each other."

I nodded, thinking of my mother and Grandad, of some of the stories Baby had told me. "Except you're scared," I said. "And he isn't."

She moved her head in silence, pondering this. I didn't insist. There was so much I would have liked to say, but who was I to give unsolicited advice? What did I know after the little I'd heard?

"You can stay here as long as you like."

She smiled thinly. Then she pressed her lips together and closed her eyes. "I can't believe I paid with my card." she said. "What was I thinking?"

I didn't tell her how long he'd suspected she was in Bad Heim, didn't say that he'd been calling for days and must have called all their friends too. I wondered what she'd talked about with Baby, but she seemed tired, so I didn't ask.

"He only knows you're in Bad Heim," I reminded her. "He doesn't know you're here in the hotel."

She looked at me as if she weren't so sure—as if it were unlikely I'd managed to deceive him. "I can't hide forever. I just have to sort myself out a bit. I had to get away from the person I'd become. I was someone completely different before I met him. I played lead roles. I traveled, I had friends." She was talking to her reflection, her eyes only occasionally drifting to my face, as if by chance. "I despised women who were in what seemed like unequal relationships, women who stayed home with the kids. I was very quick to judge and very harsh on them. *Break up, move on. It's your own fault if you let him treat you like that.*" Again, the mirthless laugh. "He ate into my life like a cancer until I saw everything through his eyes. My acting work, my friends, my mother, myself. When I met him it was like he showed me this fenced-in area and said: Look, that's you in that pathetic little garden and you think it's the whole world. I wanted out. Out of that life, away from the constant financial worries. I thought he had something better to offer. Ease. Security." She paused, then went on. "We had it good at first. A lovely apartment, vacations. No more pressure. I didn't have to take every role I was offered, didn't have to worry about where the next part was coming from. I wasn't at the mercy of directors anymore, the industry. But then it got to the point where it was just him and me and eventually Ilya. Everything else was gone."

A cough came from the bed, the sound of someone rolling over. Dori went to check on Ilya, then reappeared in the door. "I'm sorry, Iris. I've taken far too much of your time."

I pressed her hand when I left, hoping she knew I was on her side, that she was safe in the hotel.

Outside, a warm wind was blowing through the maple, rippling the pond. A big fish was floating on the surface, tossed by the choppy water.

8

The wind got up in the night, exacerbating the situation in the forest. The flames were unpredictable during the gusts, and if the wildfire reached the treetops there was a risk that everything would spiral out of control. In the prolonged heat the vegetation had lost so much moisture that the firefighters were struggling to keep pace. Planes flew over the hotel at regular intervals, trailing their shadows through the gray garden. On the warning app the color-coded zones swept across the map, growing darker. I was googling the latest changes to the regulations when the phone rang.

"You never got back to me."

One day. He'd given me one day.

"Are you following the news on Bad Heim?" I asked.

"Of course."

I thought of the plan Dori and I had made. We would leave the hotel early that evening and drive as far as we could. Train service at Bad Heim was suspended, but there were still trains running a few towns away. Dori wanted to get as far from Bad Heim as possible and buy a ticket to Düsseldorf or Leipzig from a vending machine. She'd lived—and acted—in both places. She would pay with her card, making her husband think she'd moved on. Then we'd drive back to the hotel, hoping he'd follow the false trail.

"I'm afraid I don't have time to make inquiries for you," I said. "There are mass evacuations underway here. I have to get ready."

This was an exaggeration, but I thought it would make my story more plausible.

"What does that mean for you exactly?" He sounded as if he might offer to help.

"It means I have to pack. Figure out what can go in the fire storage cabinet and what has to come with me."

Although he was as polite as ever, I found myself struggling to suppress the coldness that had crept into my voice. He was silent for a moment, then put his finger right on the button.

"Something's different about you," he said, calm and controlled.

"As I said, things here are very fraught."

"Your voice has changed."

"I really don't have time," I said curtly.

He was silent again.

"I understand," he said at length. I would have liked

to hang up, but he kept me on the line. "As I'm sure you can imagine, my concerns have been deepened by the developments in Bad Heim."

I did my best to sound friendly. I thought of the lie I'd told and asked myself what I'd say if things were really the way I was pretending they were. "I appreciate that," I said. "But I'm afraid I can't help you. I have such a lot to do."

"I believe you. I've seen the news. I don't want to keep you. It's just—are you sure you haven't heard anything that might have a bearing on my problem?" When I didn't reply he went on. "If you knew my wife as I do, you'd know why I'm so insistent. My hands are tied, do you understand? It's hard from a distance. My wife makes a strong impression on people and she takes advantage of that. She can be very disarming, you know. Very attractive. She's beautiful, she's calm and collected. It's easy to overlook what's behind the façade. You mustn't let her lead you astray."

I forced a laugh, hoping it sounded natural. "We're not allowed out at the moment, so I'm in no danger of being led astray by your wife." Into the silence that followed, I wished him all the best.

"You too," he said. "Good luck with your preparations." Then: "Just one last thing. My wife doesn't lie, I'm not saying that, but she's an actress. Did I already mention that? My wife's a very good actress—it's second nature to her, do you understand?"

He went on talking and I let him.

"She's a good mother too, as long as she's stable. I'm not questioning that, don't get me wrong. But nothing goes deep with her, do you understand? Everything's precarious, it can change from one moment to the next. I would ask you to bear that in mind if you do come across her or happen to hear anything. What you see, the way she presents, is only the surface. My wife is mentally unfit. She has a personality disorder. It's important to be clear about that."

I could feel his words working on me. How well did I know Dori? I thought of her face, the slight tremor in her eyebrow, at the corner of her mouth. I thought of her gaze, of her hand in mine.

"Let me give you an example," the man said calmly. "She jumped down a flight of stairs with our daughter. Can you imagine? Quite steep stone stairs, with a baby. And that's just one example—I could give you plenty of others."

I thought of Dori's version. Of her short white tooth close to my face. *He just keeps on and on and on and on.* No mention of Ilya.

"It was pure luck they survived. Pure luck."

Images kept flashing into my head, as if the stories I'd heard—the glimpses into these strangers' marriage— were scenes from a movie. Dori on the stairs with Ilya, Dori on her way back from the supermarket. I didn't understand how she could have let her husband treat her like that, why she'd stayed so long. The only thing I was sure of was that Dori had been right to leave. *We bring out the worst in each other.*

"My wife is in Bad Heim," the man went on. "As you say yourself, the situation's getting worse. My daughter is there. I don't want to hassle you, but I'm helpless, do you understand? My wife can't cope on her own and there's nothing I can do. She does what she wants, takes my little girl to a wildfire region, and there's nothing I can do."

I told him I understood and that, should it come to an evacuation, I'd keep a lookout for a stranger with a child. I told him that was all I could offer.

Although I'd made things sound worse than they were, the situation had definitely changed. The heat had intensified, restrictions were tighter, the planes flew more frequently. The fires were louder, more present. Smoke hung thick over the field in the red-tinged air. The big dead fish was in the garbage can; the others lurked beneath the murky surface of the warm pond. Ash and embers were everywhere, and the leaves of the red maple had curled up like caterpillars, hard and black at the edges. I felt as if I were standing in a field of wheat, watching a gathering storm. Soon the storm would sweep away everything around me, but for the moment there were only the massing clouds and the wheat swaying in the wind.

For the moment we were staying put.

Dori and I peeled potatoes; we bathed Ilya; in the dim light of the dining room we pushed three armchairs in front of the TV under one of the fans. I watched Dori's still face in the flicker of the screen—her smile, her shoulders. Sometimes our eyes met and she laughed; it felt like a long time since I'd lived here alone. I noticed how calmly she talked to Ilya. I compared what I saw with what the man had told me.

Mentally unfit. Personality disorder.

It was quiet where we were. Cartoons and cornflakes—and out there the fire.

I sat on the cool tiles with Ilya and showed her the Barbie suitcase house—how to turn the fireplace into a bookcase and the table into a bed.

I scrolled through real estate offers, always coming to the same conclusion: neither the hotel nor the land it was on was worth anything anymore, and I didn't have enough savings to buy elsewhere. There was no question of uprooting and starting again. Dori leaned over the arm of my chair and looked over my shoulder. I felt my own body every time she came close to me—felt my T-shirt moving with my breath. There was one place that particularly appealed to us, a little bed-and-breakfast with a view of a lake. Dori knew the area; she'd once auditioned in a small-town theater there. "They made me an offer, but I turned it down." She laughed. "Maybe they'd take me now."

"You want to start acting again?" I asked. It was the first time she'd hinted at a future, given me a glimpse of her plans. We scrolled through the photo gallery: the little rooms, the surroundings. Green woods, mountains, the lake at sunrise. A kindergarten, a primary school.

Ilya sat between us with the dollhouse, as if she were at the bottom of a pond. Stacking little plastic plates, running her finger over the bright-pink wallpaper, the cracked foil of the tiny mirror.

There were 430,000 euros between us and this other life. Playing with Ilya in the sitting room while Dori was busy with rehearsals and performances. Watching Ilya in the garden with other children. Making my rounds of the little rooms. Open windows, fresh air, walks by the lake. We laughed about it. "He'd never find us there," Dori whispered, her face close to mine.

We set off toward evening. It was still unbearable outside—searing heat under a bell jar of smoke. The wind seemed barely to move the air, only pressing it hot against our skin, into every crevice, stinging our eyes, burning our throats with every breath. We stuck to the car seats; everything seemed to have turned strangely viscous—the imitation leather, the asphalt. Everything felt soft. The steering wheel was so hot I had to wear the thin cotton gloves I kept in the car for that purpose.

We drove through town onto the highway, Dori on the passenger seat, Ilya in the back, under a silver emergency blanket. I felt my T-shirt wet against my back. I felt sweat trickle along my thighs, into the clammy hollows of my knees, and down to my ankles. In the footwell next to Dori's legs was a cooler of ice cubes, damp towels, and a big bottle of water.

I'd expected a certain amount of traffic, but soon realized I'd underestimated the number of people leaving the area. As the sun began to set, we found ourselves almost at a standstill, in a long line of cars packed to the brim with belongings. Tired, gray children's faces behind green-tinted sun protection film. Lolling bodies swathed in silver, battery fans and old-school paper fans, washrags mopping faces and necks. There was no other way of keeping cool in the cars. The high toxicity levels meant that air-conditioning and ventilation systems had to stay switched off and windows closed.

There was no turning for miles. At first Ilya cried; then she sat quietly slumped in her seat. I asked Dori if she'd had enough to drink. Dori pulled a small, half-full plastic bottle from her purse and handed it to her.

In the rearview mirror, a wall of smoke rose behind the cars following us. I saw that Dori was also drenched in sweat, her neck damp, her dress spotted with dark patches.

"I don't have much," she said. "I didn't know we'd be out this long."

I apologized to her. I always forgot that she wasn't as good at gauging the situation as I was. "It'll be enough. It cools down when it gets dark."

The worst of the heat went away at sunset, but the thermometer dropped slowly: 109 ... 108.5 ... 108 ... I noticed that Dori was getting nervous. We were at a total standstill, the sweat pouring off us. Ilya looked exhausted. Dori kept swiveling around to her, telling her to drink, asking her questions, reaching under the emergency blanket. "She's soaked," she said. "Completely soaked."

I asked if she wanted to turn back, and suggested taking the next exit. We hadn't gone fifteen miles from Bad Heim.

"I don't know." I noticed she was avoiding eye contact. She reached around with frenzied movements, swapping Ilya's blanket for a cool towel, wiping the sweat from her legs and face. "I need to get her out of these things," she said. "They're sopping wet." She tugged at the damp clothes. Ilya had closed her eyes.

I couldn't figure it out. Was she angry at me? Did she regret setting off? Did she think I should have been more responsible, taken a more realistic view? I felt suddenly interfering and naïve—too involved in a plan that hardly concerned me. I knew nothing of her life, her responsibilities. And yet I thought I knew better. I believed I had a firmer grip on reality, a clearer idea of what was to be done. I thought of my mother and Grandad, of Dori's husband. I was engaging in exactly the same behavior that I condemned in others, trying to take the situation out of Dori's hands, trying to take the child out of her hands—but at the same time, wasn't that what she was asking for?

Then Dori tried to wet the towel with cold water, and the big glass bottle slipped from her damp hands and rolled into the back footwell.

"Careful!" I said, a little too loudly. I felt anger rise in me; I wanted to be alone. It was all getting to be too much—the heat, the traffic jam, Dori's jumpiness. She was rummaging for the bottle, her hip pressed against my shoulder. Too close, too warm. I asked her if she'd spilled any, making an effort to sound calm. No answer. She went on rubbing Ilya's body, dabbing pointlessly at her lips with water.

"She won't wake up," she said shrilly. "I can't get her to wake up."

It was only then I realized she was crying, saw the blotches on her neck, realized she'd almost lost control of her hands. Ilya was lying on the back seat in only her panties, her skin yellow and clammy, unresponsive to her mother's attempts to rouse her.

I asked again if she'd had enough to drink during the day. I hadn't been keeping tabs myself. Dori didn't reply. She was shaking Ilya, trying to prop her up in the seat. Next to Dori's wet thigh I switched from first to second gear as the line of cars began to inch forward. It was dark now. A long trail of red lights stretched into the distance ahead; behind us, headlamps beamed through the smoke as far as the eye could see.

"Shall I take the next exit?" I asked. "Shall we drive to the hospital?"

Dori called Ilya's name in a panic, over and over, and in between times she cried out, half to me, half to herself, "She's not reacting. She's not reacting."

Somehow she managed to pull the child's limp body to the front of the car and onto her lap; she clasped it tight, as if afraid it might slide, wet and heavy, out of her grasp—the skinny arms and legs, the neck, the head: a slippery bundle of floppy limbs and joints. Dori tried to give Ilya water from the big bottle. I saw that the child had opened her eyes, but her head lolled in the crook of Dori's arm as if she couldn't hold it up anymore.

"Do you have any glucose?" I asked. I'd heard that glucose and sports drinks were good for dehydration.

"No, I don't have any glucose!" she screamed. "It wasn't my idea to go on this crazy journey! I had no idea what I was getting myself into!"

I was familiar with this—the mood swings, the accusations. It was like hearing my mother talk in Dori's voice, overwhelmed by everything. I couldn't expect her to make decisions.

"I'm driving to the hospital."

"Not the hospital! We can't go to the hospital!"

I said nothing. I took off my gloves and felt my damp, spongy fingertips on the hot plastic. I rifled through the glove box and my purse for old candy or gum, but without any luck.

Eventually we reached the exit and then the next town. I stopped without comment at the only pharmacy that was open and described Ilya's symptoms through a little window.

"You must take her to the emergency room," the pharmacist said, an elderly woman with red hair and red-framed glasses, her face serious on the other side of the perforated window. "You need to get her looked at." She asked when Ilya had last eaten and drunk, had she vomited, what color was her skin, the whites of her eyes? "If she's not reacting she might be dehydrated and then she'd definitely need an IV. If it's smoke in her lungs that's more serious. You need to take her straight to the hospital."

I asked if there was anything we could give her on the way, and the pharmacist sold me a baby bottle and an electrolyte powder that she mixed with water for me in a back room. I ran back to the car, gave Dori the bottle of electrolyte solution, and put the name of a children's clinic I had gotten from the pharmacist into the GPS. Dori's hands trembled as she tried to push the teat between Ilya's lips.

"Is she drinking?"

No answer.

"Is she drinking?" I was shouting now, helpless with worry.

Ilya lay in Dori's arms like a baby, her long pale legs folded against the window. Dori said something in a fast, panicky whisper; I couldn't make out a word. She put up no resistance when I pulled up outside the hospital and took Ilya from her arms.

9

We spent the night there. It was cool and bright and astonishingly quiet, considering the number of people. The corridors were full of soft, limp bodies on narrow gurneys. Tubes in nostrils, masks, drips, bandages, machines pumping and beeping. The staff looked after people in a routine, unsentimental fashion. Beside us, Ilya's small, sleeping body lay under a thin, striped sheet, a needle in the crook of her arm. Carbs, salts, and liquids dripped through a tube into her blood. Dori sat next to her in silence, her hand on the child's chest. I brought her coffee and a sandwich from the cafeteria.

"I'm sorry," I said. "For putting you in this situation."

"No, I'm sorry," she said. Her voice was tired. She let out a puff of air and pressed her lips together.

"Are you on your husband's insurance?" I asked. "Is that why you didn't want to come?"

She nodded. "He gets to hear everything." After a

pause she added, "He's very well connected. They're all in cahoots."

I imagined Alexander Vargas at a table with the health insurance people, other doctors, lawyers, judges. I saw them shaking hands, laughing together, exchanging stories and privileges. I thought of the way he'd tried to rope me into his plans, offered me money.

She shrugged. "Maybe it's for the best."

I'd given her a brief account of my last phone call with her husband that afternoon, talking in a hushed voice in the kitchen while Ilya watched TV. Now I thought back with shame to the energy we'd felt, the childish delight we'd taken in our escapade. We'd been so proud of our plan, naïvely believing we could outsmart Alexander Vargas and all that he stood for. That had been a mistake, and what was worse, it had blinded us to the danger posed by the fires, especially to Ilya. I thought of how I'd relished her silence, her sleepiness— the chance to spend time alone with Dori, to laugh with her, find out more about her.

Now nothing was left of our hopes. We'd neglected Ilya's well-being. We'd harmed her. What a harebrained idea it had been. And how outrageous, how stupid of us to put it into practice. I felt responsible. I'd interfered in Dori's life. I'd thoughtlessly urged her to follow through a dangerous, futile plan, and I felt uneasily that my motives had been selfish. I'd wanted to keep her and Ilya with me at any price, though I knew so little about them or their circumstances.

I asked Dori about the time she'd jumped down the stairs. Had she been holding Ilya?

There was a line of smudged makeup around her nose and mouth, blue rings under her eyes. Her hair had dried in rats' tails; her dress was stained with white sweat marks. She didn't hesitate or attempt to hide anything. Yes, she'd jumped with her—Ilya had been in the baby carrier at the time. I put my hand on hers, on the cold fist that lay in her lap beside the shrink-wrapped sandwich.

"I didn't realize till it was too late. That I wasn't alone—that she was with me."

Dori looked at me. I felt her hand tense up beneath mine.

She told me how her husband had taken care of her afterward. How he'd driven her to the hospital without a cross word. She told me of the weeks spent waiting for her arms to mend. The first days when he'd looked after her and Ilya single-handedly, then the six weeks when her mother had come to live with them. Dori's husband had examined Dori every evening after work; he'd cut up her food for her; he'd bought her a long straw so she could drink without using her hands.

Those late summer days were happy days. His hand on her leg as they talked after dinner when Ilya had been put to bed. Then movies on TV, the curtains over the bed billowing into the room in the night wind, the smell of fall.

"I was so naïve. So naïve. I really thought things were different. I thought he'd realized we'd both gone

too far—that things had to change. All that drama before I jumped—the shouting, the insults. And Ilya between us all the way through—in the baby carrier, right
over my beating heart. I was so caught up in the situation, the fight, that I forgot all about her. I can't even
remember if she was awake or not—if she cried. It was
only afterward—the day after the cast came off, when
we got back from seeing my mother onto the train—that
I realized none of it had been real; he'd been faking it for
weeks. He stood there in the door. I was trying to take
Ilya's shoes off, laughing at how thin and puny my arms
were after so long in plaster. And he didn't even react.
His eyes were cold.

"I went over to him. I said, 'Is everything okay?'

"And he said, 'A woman like you shouldn't have a
child.' Just like that. In front of Ilya. She was sitting between us playing with her shoes. I felt like he'd pushed
me into an abyss. All those weeks of being cared for
by him—and then suddenly to realize that he'd been
judging me all along. I tried to talk to him, but all he'd
say was that I could count myself lucky if he continued
to tolerate me in her presence. And he was right. I lost
control. Mothers can't do that."

I ran my fingers over her cold, white knuckles and
asked what he'd meant.

"That he can take her away from me if he wants to."
Her voice cracked as she spoke; she could hardly get the
words out.

"He can't do that—" I said, but she interrupted me.

"I jumped down the stairs with her, Iris. My broken bones, her bruises—it's all documented."

I felt myself losing her, felt the panic rise in her. I remembered her outcry in the car, her tears. How little I understood her situation. How much her thoughts and decisions must be affected by her fear of losing the child.

"I'm sorry I brought you here," I said. "Maybe I can do something. Maybe we can get them to stop the insurance company from disclosing your data to him. There must be some form of protection."

"I shouldn't have run away with her," she said. "I've only made it worse. I have to go back to him sometime; he won't wait forever."

I hugged her. We didn't speak. For now, we were sitting here. It was cool, and Ilya had all she needed. This thing that was my life was only a window in time for Dori, a temporary extension of the leash her husband kept her on. One of these days he would haul it in, and it wouldn't just be him at the other end but all his capital, people he could pay to bend reality to his desires. Dori, meanwhile, at her end, was all alone. Apart from me, of course—but what good was I to her?

Later she told me she'd spent weeks—months—trying to win him back. Apologizing, making promises. Always the same question: What can I do? How can I show you that I can change, that I can do things better? But no response.

"How long did that go on for?"

She shrugged. "A couple of years. Until the end. Until I left."

I pictured a house in a beautiful, rich neighborhood. White walls, elegant, expensive furniture, an impeccable lawn behind french windows. I saw a man and woman walking through the rooms without speaking, Ilya between them. Dori in one of her lovely dresses, her hair falling over her shoulders in a perfect line, her smooth, made-up face.

I squeezed her hand. In the scene I imagined, she seemed transparent, without substance, as if a puff of air would blow her away.

"You're out of all that now, you and Ilya. Things can only get better."

She avoided looking at me. "I wasn't prepared today. Didn't pack any food, didn't pack enough water, forgot to keep an eye on her drinking, didn't stop to think what it would be like in the car in that heat."

"Look," I said. "She's doing well."

We were sitting on cool, pale-pink plastic chairs, Dori's legs next to mine, our reflection in a pane of milk glass opposite, our hands in Dori's lap. Ilya lay beside us, under a stiff sheet, cool and cared for.

I told Dori about my childhood—about times that sounded like poverty and instability and chaos, but only taken as a whole. The details told a different story. A tent of sheets in a hostel dorm. Entire gâteaux given to us for free by a baker after closing time. Apples and plums gathered from suburban sidewalks—and my mother, who could make a game out of anything. I talked about her as if those periods of energy were all she'd known, and kept quiet about the rest.

Dori smiled. After a while we fell silent. Lush green plants were dotted about, in the corridors, between the beds, among the islands of chairs. Ferns, weeping figs, fiddle-leaf figs—they cast tall shadows in the fluorescent light. It was only hours later, when a full three infusion bags had run into Ilya's body, that I noticed that they, too, were plastic.

Later, in a low voice, Dori told me of her insomnia, of wandering the house at night, trying to remove all traces of the day. Wiping the surfaces, sweeping the floors, scooping muesli out of the drain. She told me that her husband had sold her car without telling her. That she'd started to take his car out at night, because driving was the only thing that calmed her. Through the neighborhood, onto the highway, right out of town.

"I always turned back in the end. And I never took Ilya with me. I used to count the years and tell myself I'd just have to put up with it until she was grown-up. Better than being without her, better than going back to eking out a living on the breadline. I wanted it for Ilya; it was her childhood, after all. The garden, the nice neighborhood—it was all part of it."

A doctor came. She checked Ilya's pulse and took blood from her finger. Everything was looking good. We should let Ilya sleep and wait for the last drip to finish. Then we could go home.

When the doctor moved on to the next bed, Dori went on as if there had been no interruption. She spoke of the accumulation of circumstances leading to her departure. Ilya asking why Daddy could hear her when he couldn't hear Dori, caught in bewilderment between her parents. Alexander's silence, his habit of ignoring Dori when she spoke to him, the manipulative remarks he made to Ilya. Then Dori's mother's death, the return to her mother's apartment to go through the old, familiar things, two weeks alone with Ilya in the empty rooms, back in her old life. Evenings on a folding chair, reading and rereading Ada Lumin, brief chats with a neighbor on the stairs, the anxious countdown as the last day approached. It had become increasingly clear to Dori that she couldn't go back—and in the end it was easy. A matter of catching a different train.

"My mother was very fond of Alexander. He's a charmer—knows how to make anyone like him; she saw it as a real achievement that I'd married a man like that. I couldn't have brought myself to tell her how bad things were after she left. Couldn't have told her he'd stopped speaking to me. Or that he'd moved into the guest room—that he didn't want me anymore, that he'd stopped looking at me, stopped touching me."

She shrugged and fell quiet. After her mother's sudden death she'd had to clear out her apartment, wrap up her life, eliminate all traces of it. The ashtray, the lipsticks with their weirdly sloping tips, bottles of nail polish, blister packs, her footprints in a pair of silver mules. The order, the cleanliness, the minutiae of domestic organization. Dozens of plastic containers—one filled with those little wire ties that come on bags of sliced bread, one with barrettes, another with sachets of sugar and sweetener. A whole apartment full of useless things.

"I put everything in garbage bags, everything. Clothes, scarves, books, photo albums, wooden spoons, knives—the lot. I paid someone to come and take it away, and two days later it was all gone. I only hung on to the things Ilya and I actually needed: the mattress, the TV, the fridge, the washing machine, the balcony furniture. Every evening I texted Alexander to tell him I needed more time. I invented reasons for the delay. In fact, the apartment was long since empty. We stayed two weeks." Dori told me about the little red marks she'd noticed when she cleaned the kitchen for the next tenants. In the fridge, on the light switch, on the washing machine. She'd scrubbed and scrubbed, but couldn't get them off, and eventually she realized that they were from her mother's polished nails—that her mother had been leaving those marks around the apartment all her life. With every move she'd made, every carton of milk she'd gotten out of the fridge, every load of laundry she'd done. "And now they were all that was left of her. I couldn't get my head round it."

Eventually, she said, she couldn't stick it out in the apartment any longer. She texted Alexander. *Home tomorrow.* She spent a last evening on the plastic chair while Ilya slept on the mattress. By then someone had come for the TV; the suitcase was packed and ready in the hall. Dori sat by the window and that line came back to her. *He eats me up till nothing's left.* She felt suddenly hot and nauseated and her heart thumped until her whole body trembled. She told herself it was only until Ilya was grown-up, a finite period of time. She saw her life with Alexander as a string of beads that she would slowly unstring, one bead at a time. But when she got to the station the next day, she didn't take the Berlin train. She took the train to Munich and from there to Bad Heim.

10

Ilya was discharged in the early morning. I'd spoken to a woman at reception and pleaded Dori's case, painting a dramatic picture of her predicament. To my surprise, the woman deleted our data from the system and waved us through; she didn't even look up from her screen. I put ten euros in the backside of a china pig labeled *Coffee Kitty*, and we left the building.

Ilya was better, her cheeks red. She held a stuffed animal on her lap that Dori had bought her in the little hospital kiosk.

We parked at the station. Dori bought a ticket to Düsseldorf at the ticket machine and paid by card. We'd made it.

It was a little cooler—bearable; the display on the platform read *32 °C, Dienstag, der 19. Oktober, 07:12.* The road to Bad Heim was almost empty.

The sun was rising behind white smoke. We headed

for town, driving into a milky landscape of bright-pink light.

We listened to music. It was the first time I'd seen Dori relaxed and uninhibited. I saw her gesture expansively; I heard her voice when she sang.

Her husband would know nothing of Ilya's night in the hospital. He wouldn't come to Bad Heim. She was no longer alone; she had time.

Billy Idol was playing on the radio. "White Wedding." Dori sang along. Then she turned to me and said, "Everything's so easy with you!" She laughed as she spoke, her short tooth glinting in the light. "We'll get married, and Ilya and I will stay on with you."

"We'll buy the lakeside B and B," I said. "And you can act at the local theater."

For a moment it seemed possible.

We laughed, we sang, we drove.

A landscape of light.

We stopped at the wholesale store to stock up on food; Ilya rode up and down the long, air-conditioned aisles in the shopping cart with her stuffed animal. Back at the hotel we set up camp in the dining room. It was the biggest, coolest room in the building, and on the doctor's advice we'd decided to use it as a bedroom for the three of us—at least as long as the extreme heat continued. Dori and I dragged mattresses into place and fetched what we needed from our rooms, moving as quickly as we could through the smoke and heat. Our eyes immediately started to water; we coughed despite our masks.

Ilya lay on her mattress; we'd changed her pillowcase and washed her pajamas. She was still exhausted and needed rest, plenty to drink, and light food with lots of salt or sugar. I sat with her for a while, telling her more stories about the little girls and the talking dog, making up new adventures for them in a world that wasn't on fire. We set the timer on my phone and woke her every two hours to give her spoonfuls of broth and cold sweet tea, tiny quantities of rice, fish, blancmange.

Damp sheets over washing lines divided the room into cool white tents. The fans were running; the TV was on low. On the local news it looked as if we wouldn't have to evacuate; the river was continuing to act as a buffer. We just had to wait, bide our time until the rain came.

Outside everything was white, gray, brown. Smoke everywhere. My red maple was barely visible, little more than a shape moving in the wind. We kept the windows and curtains closed and spent the day in the dining room. It was like being at the bottom of a deep lake.

The TV broadcast images of other rescue zones. Hundreds of people on folding stretchers. Big silver AC units in basements and gymnasiums.

We drank iced tea with our feet in the tub and gave Ilya our ice cubes to suck. Neither Dori nor I had slept the night before. We were exhausted—by the persistent heat, the drive, the bad air. If we moved too quickly, the world disappeared behind patches of black. Dori complained of headaches and nausea. I brought her peppermint oil, cold compresses, water. In between times I saw her take various other meds—drops and pills that she kept in her toiletry bag. We nodded off, woke again, waited. The day—our life—in two-hour slots.

When Dori and Ilya were asleep, I sat alone on my mattress in front of the TV. Sweaty reporters in dirty masks appeared on the screen, their arms gray. Flames surged like a wave through the forest, or what was left of it. Spindly black trunks. There was a lot of footage of the climate camp. In the red-hot inferno the tents melted into grotesque shapes within seconds, collapsed, burst into flame. The long banner calling for a limit of 3.2-degrees Fahrenheit flicked up like a tongue and vanished from the picture. I thought of the young activists and wondered where they were. I imagined the belongings they'd left behind: sleeping bags, tins of food, bamboo toothbrushes, a guitar. In the end, I thought, what little the fire had spared would lie there in the cold ash, black and destroyed.

I kept getting news alerts on my phone; our fire was in the national headlines again. People I hadn't heard from for years suddenly checked in with me, asking about the hotel, about the situation in Bad Heim.

In the afternoon, Paula called. She sounded worried. I stood between the sheets and spoke in whispers, trying to reassure her. She was planning to come to Bad Heim to fetch her mother. "You should leave too, Iris," she said. "You're always welcome here, you know that."

After we'd hung up I put on a clean mask and went out the glass door, into the garden. The heat shot through my body to my head, roaring in my ears, smarting on my skin. I could feel the hot gravel through the soles of my flip-flops, the rubber softening and sticking with every step. I unrolled the garden hose—that, too, soft and hot—and turned on the water. I let it run for a long time, until it had cooled to lukewarm and eventually to cold. Then I pulled the hose over the gravel and through the smoke toward the pond. I could hardly keep my eyes open. Somewhere, I thought, I had a pair of pale-blue goggles—it was time I looked for them. I hunkered down. Only a puddle of hot water was left at the bottom of the pond. The fish lay still on the black plastic lining, shimmering gold beneath the smoke, their eyes a murky pale blue. One of them had burst and was oozing innards, all a blur through my watering eyes. It was only now, from this crouched position, that I noticed the birds, the starlings. Soft dead bodies on the hot gravel around the edge of the pond. Fifteen, twenty, thirty—hard to say. I imagined them covering the garden to the fence, strewn across the field to the forest. Hundreds of them, their feathers ruffled in the wind. At some point I'd have to gather them up. I pictured myself with the shovel, scooping up the little corpses and dumping them in a blue garbage bag. I watered the tree, aiming the jet of water at the trunk and branches for minutes at a time. Maybe it would survive.

Early that evening two girls turned up at the hotel. I heard their voices through the labyrinth of sheets separating our camp from reception, but I was so sleepy and the sounds of the TV and the firefighting planes were so distracting that it was a while before I recognized the girls' *Hello?* and *Is anyone there?* as the calls of people seeking refuge.

I glanced at the mattress where Ilya and Dori lay sleeping, Dori's arm over Ilya's chest, Ilya's hair on Dori's hand. They were breathing softly; now and then Ilya coughed in her sleep. I got up and made my way to the entrance. Two young women were standing there. I put them in their early twenties if not younger. One of them was the short-haired woman I'd seen interviewed on TV. Their eyes were red and swollen. They had no luggage, except for small fanny packs slung across their chests—containing, I guessed, their most important documents and maybe some cash. The girl from the interview had an empty glass bottle in her hand. I noticed her short nails, her little tattoos. I saw the dirty red marks left by the face masks that now hung from their elbows. Their clothes—shorts, T-shirts, sneakers—were stained and gray, as were their arms and legs. Everything about them seemed to be covered in an oily film, a mixture of sweat, soot, and dust.

I was surprised at how high their voices were. They spoke rapidly, politely, eloquently, and sounded younger than on TV. They asked tentatively if it was possible for them to stay in the hotel until their parents came for them in the morning. They had twelve euros between them, they said. How much did a room cost? I waved this aside. They thanked me and asked if they could get washed. I took keys from reception and fetched two clean masks, two thin hotel bathrobes, and two little toiletry sets: soap, Q-tips, toothpaste, and a toothbrush. We all put on masks. I opened the terrace door a crack and we slipped out into the heat.

The wooden boards of the veranda were warm and creaked underfoot. Flakes of ash rose and fell in the tepid wind like dead moths. The smoke now came right up to the building. We groped our way to the first door, our eyes barely open. Everything was hot beneath my fingers—the wall, the handle, the door. I could feel the paint peeling, could feel every part of the building succumbing to the heat. I pushed the girls into the room, closed the door, and kicked a rolled-up blanket against the gap at the bottom, but even so, everything smelled of smoke. I explained to the girls that we'd taken our mattresses into the dining room and would later set up camp for them there too. It wasn't safe in the annex. I told them how long they could shower and left my watch with them so they could keep an eye on the time.

Back in the main building I prepared a light meal for them. I guessed they wouldn't eat meat, or indeed any animal products. It occurred to me they might have had issues with the disposable toiletry sets I'd given them, but if so, they hadn't let it show.

When they came back, they were wearing the bathrobes. I took their clothes and carried them through the kitchen to the laundry room. There was a ban on washing machines because of water regulations, so I put the dirty things in the sink with some water, added washing powder, and kneaded suds into the clothes until the water was a murky brown. When everything was clean I wrung it out and hung it over the lines in the dining room, between the cooling sheets.

Fresh from the shower, the girls looked even younger, their faces soft and unlined. I took them iced tea, tomato salad, cold soup, and bread.

The TV reports from the forest drifted quietly across the room from Ilya and Dori's camp. I hoped they'd stay asleep and recover their strength a bit—especially Dori.

"Like to join us?" The girls smiled at me and pointed to an empty chair at their table. This youthful solidarity was strange to me, the girls' easy familiarity, the care with which they treated each other, their openness toward me. There was something gentle and thoughtful about them; their interest was genuine.

"Nice safe space you've got here," said the longer-haired girl, who had introduced herself as Cleo.

"Feels weird sitting at a table again, doesn't it?" the other one—Lou—remarked. They both laughed. They'd had to vacate the camp the night before.

"I'm sorry you had to leave everything behind," I said. "I saw your tents on TV."

They seemed to feel no grief. They'd known all along that it was only a matter of time before the fires reached the camp.

"I've been following your work all summer—the banners, the slogans, the protests."

They laughed again. "It must be hard living here. We only work in precarious places like this for short periods." They raised their shoulders and looked at me with something like pity—not just for me but for all those with ties to Bad Heim or the forest. They talked of their work as activists, explaining that they'd have to return to the wildfire zone as soon as they could to clear up what was left of the camp.

"It's especially tragic here," one of them said. "The way the ecosystem just collapsed."

I asked what she meant. She spoke about ecological dynamics, about the reasons why rejuvenation wasn't possible in the Bad Heim forest, why nature had lost its power to retaliate against the fires.

"That's why we're in Bad Heim," the other said. "It's so in-your-face here. A couple of decades ago this was a major vacation hotspot—now the place is dead. I know it sounds awful, but that makes it a great backdrop for us. Maybe seeing us on TV with our message will trigger something in people. Maybe they'll realize how urgent things are."

"Urgent." They laughed. "Actually, it's already too late."

It was well into the evening when Dori joined us. She looked sleepy, surprised at the visitors, maybe also a little dazed from her meds. She made several attempts to light her cigarette, then sat down with us and followed the conversation without contributing to it. I went to fetch her something to eat.

When I came back she was listening to the girls with interest. It was a side of her I hadn't seen before. I was surprised how much she knew about the activists' work and how critical she was of the situation in Bad Heim. I was reminded of the time she'd asked what I planned to do when the region was no longer inhabitable.

The three of them were deep in conversation, but they immediately included me when I sat down.

"Cleo's been explaining that in our movement, there's a certain potential for conflict, despite the fact we're all on the same ideological page. Yeah? Is that a fair way of putting it?"

Nodding and laughter.

"Not between us, of course."

"No way!"

Their hands brushing each other, their shoulders touching, their teeth straight and white. "The thing is"—turning to us again—"there are always these people who see it more like an adventure, who are only in it for the drama. Nothing wrong with that, of course—we need to keep the numbers up; everyone has a function. It's just hard when you can't one-hundred-percent rely on people. Isn't it?"

"Yeah, totally. The situation's too risky for that."

I sensed a difference between these women and me, but found it hard to put my finger on it. I was familiar with some of the issues from the internet, but I'd never heard anyone talk like this before. They threw words around like *petromasculinity* and *fossil capitalism*; their language was quietly and effortlessly woke. They made me feel old-fashioned; I suddenly felt the need to justify my passivity, my reluctance to leave the hotel.

"Maybe you're just too close to it all," Lou said to me. "We see that a lot. People who are where the action is can't step back and see what's going on, what needs doing."

Cleo nodded. Although there were only about ten or fifteen years separating the girls from Dori and me, I felt very old next to them—old and inflexible.

"It's absurd, of course, that individuals have to assume this responsibility, but there's no way existing structures can be deconstructed without a broad social basis."

A broad social basis—that meant everyone. Solidarity. Responsibility. There were concrete plans for action and change. The longer I talked with these young women, the more I felt not only shame but also a sense that everything hung in the balance. That these girls and their comrades in arms were at the root of a movement that was about so much more than the situation in our forest. It was about the gender perspective, about consumerism, personal responsibility, sexuality, social structures. The girls looked at these issues in a way that was totally new to me but second nature to them. Everything seemed fluid; they seemed to have torn everything apart with the aim of reconfiguring it, readjusting it, adapting it to a new and better future. I watched Lou and Cleo exchange glances and wondered what their relationship was.

Dori got up to check on Ilya. When she came back she'd put up her hair; her cheeks were pink. She smoked and laughed, leaning across the table to Lou and Cleo.

"You have a daughter?" Cleo asked. She and Lou smiled at Dori.

Dori drew on her cigarette. Nodded.

"That must be a mega responsibility, no?"

I remembered the evening when we'd looked at the photos together and Dori had talked for the first time about being a mother. She looked different now. More relaxed. More open.

"How do you do it? How do you raise a kid in times like these?" There was no judgment in their questions—only the desire to hear new ideas.

"The thing about having a child is that you can basically only react. You're always a step behind. No matter how good your intentions, things never quite turn out the way you want." Dori paused. "Not with me, anyway. I guess I just try not to make too many mistakes."

I thought of her leap down the stairs. Her trembling hands in the car. I looked at her. There was no tension now; her face was soft. She laughed again.

"I wouldn't have had a child if I'd known what I was letting myself in for."

I wanted to steer the conversation in a different direction, but the girls were looking at Dori with interest.

"That is so completely fascinating. Maternal love is, like, this crazy social construct. And it's totally taboo."

Dori nodded. "You can't really imagine it until you have a child of your own. It makes you unfree to an extent I hadn't anticipated. Completely dependent on another person's well-being." After a pause, she added, "It can really take it out of you."

She smiled thinly. Drew on her cigarette.

"So, do you think parenthood only works for people who've basically already opted for a certain lifestyle? Who don't feel like the setup demands sacrifices from them?"

Dori shrugged. There was a knock at the front door, and I got up to open it. Through the glass of the door I saw Baby's big body in the darkness. I let her in. She was sweating as profusely as ever, and held an open bottle of tequila in her hand as if it were a cup of coffee. She gave me a friendly slap on the shoulder as she pushed past.

"What are you girls up to?"

She saw the small party and made straight for the table, shouting things about the beauty of youth. "So this is where everyone is." She plumped down on my chair.

To my surprise Lou and Cleo greeted her as a friend, calling her by name, reaching for her free hand, smiling at her. "What are you doing here?"

I asked how they knew each other.

"Everyone knows Baby! She totally supported us in the forest!"

Baby waved this aside and yawned, showing a gold tooth and bits of food. "Here," she said. "Before I give it to the cats." She set the bottle down, stretched one of her soft, bare arms into the air and ran the other hand firmly over her hairy, wet armpit. "Didn't get you far, did it, that camp of yours." Baby leaned back, fanning air into her face. "This heat. It's apocalyptic. It'll be the death of us."

She turned to me and asked for glasses. I fetched a tray and five shot glasses from the wall closet. Nuts and olives from the kitchen. Salt, lemons, a knife. Two packs of cards from reception.

Before heading back to the others, I stood in the semidarkness, looking down the length of the dining room. How changed everything was. The dark-green curtains permanently drawn. The washing lines strung in zigzags across the room. The white sheets over them, stirring slightly in the draft of an old ceiling fan. The scattered lights, like islands in the gloaming. The flicker of the TV on the ceiling at the far end of the room. The women in the lamplight, four bodies turned to one another in the smoke, four voices—bright, dark, soft. Baby in her sleeveless blouse and long pleated skirt, snapping the elastic of her panties, rubbing her damp belly. Outside, the sirens, the firefighters, the heat.

Snatches of conversation. Dori talking about Ada Lumin's book and about her own situation. Lou and Cleo listening attentively, Cleo's hand on Dori's. Baby eager as ever to throw herself into someone else's messy life, in it for the climax, hardly able to control herself when she heard how Alexander Vargas had treated Dori after her mother had left. She slapped her thigh, tickled by his audacity, and bombarded Dori with advice. "Get rid of him," she yelled. "Don't read so much, girl. Don't spend so much time thinking."

I glanced at Dori, who laughed and added a further twist to the story. Vargas, she told us, had been out to humiliate her almost from the start of their relationship. Once, when she'd been asked to do a photo shoot for a magazine, he'd remarked that it said something about her work that she was able to make money out of photos when, objectively speaking, by today's standards, she wasn't more than seven out of ten on the scale of beauty.

"You? Seven out of ten?" Baby was scandalized and loving it.

"Because of the shape of my head," Dori explained.

"So what's he?" Lou asked.

Dori laughed and laughed; she could hardly get the words out. "He and his brother—he and his brother are nine out of ten. Objectively speaking."

When I got back to the table, Baby asked me to draw the curtains. As far as she was concerned, the topic was closed, the situation clear. Dori had left and rightly so; her only mistake had been not to go sooner. She'd given us the details, we'd had a laugh—now Baby was ready to move on.

"Can't see a damn thing. If this is coming, I want to see it. It's an inferno, I tell you! An inferno!"

Cleo stood up and drew the curtains. The darkness glowed red with pinpoints of light—a distant wall moving in billows of red and white. It sucked us in. We stood together, looking out. Silent, except for Baby's heavy breathing. I glanced at her red profile, her big old teeth. She seemed excited rather than scared.

Dori. Her cold hand next to mine.

Eventually Baby had seen enough. She called us back to the table, poured tequila, cut slices of lemon, and distributed everything like a motivated teacher. Then she raised her glass. Salt, tequila, lemon. Baby topped us up—the same again. She coughed, her black maw gaping, lemon juice dribbling down her chin. She sank back in her chair with a contented sigh and shuffled the cards. The alcohol went straight to my head. Heat and dizziness, salt and lemon.

We sat in front of the red windows playing canasta. Dori was completely focused on the game, throwing the cards down on the table and getting annoyed when things didn't go her way. In the end she won four times and was very pleased with herself. She filled everyone's glasses, and we drank.

Cleo said we needed a soundtrack and asked if we could put on some music. I realized we were being loud. Dori got up and headed to the far end of the dining room to check on Ilya again. I saw her teetering, groping her way through the now-dry sheets, struggling to find the gaps between them. I heard her laugh softly and went after her. "You okay, Dori?"

"I'm okay. Just can't find my way to Ilya." She giggled and I pointed her to the next gap—and the next, and the next. A meander through the labyrinth of bedclothes, Dori's soft face between the sheets. On one side, the murmur of serious voices and sirens from the TV; on the other, the riotous sound of Baby and the girls. We heard Baby recounting a sexual experience. We looked at each other and smiled; we were alone. Out there were the firefighters, the fire, the others, Ilya. But where we were it was still.

"I feel so good here," Dori said, suddenly very close. Her face, her cheeks, her blond hair damp at the nape of her neck.

I felt the draft from the fans, the white sheets moving around us. It was as if we were somewhere new and unfamiliar—not in the dining room, not in the hotel. I thought of the forest. Of the small, bright dome. Of the lakeside bed-and-breakfast.

Dori took a step toward me, almost losing her balance. She laughed again. I saw her little white tooth. I could smell her. Smoke, soap, tequila.

"Can you hold me?"

I held her. Her body was denser than I'd expected, her shoulders and arms firm beneath the skin. You could tell she'd had physical training. You could tell she was strong and had control of her body. She didn't melt into my embrace; she stood facing me, firm and close. I couldn't get her to lean into me. She rested her head against my neck. I ran my hands up her arms, gently stroked her hair, her shoulders. I could feel her breath on me. Then, slowly, she began to soften. Slowly, very slowly, she seemed to yield.

She put her arms around me. At first she might just have been steadying herself, but then it was really me she was holding, my body. She moved in closer, her cheek against my neck. I turned my head, touched my lips to her hair, her forehead.

Then something stirred on Ilya's side of the sheet and we moved apart.

She smiled at me. Green-gray eyes, the whites slightly bloodshot. The print of my collar on her face. "Don't go," she said. I shook my head.

She went to Ilya. I waited, listening to Dori's voice behind the sheet.

"It's all right, Ilya, it's all right, my darling. Go back to sleep. I won't be long." She paused, then went on more quietly. "Go to sleep, my darling. We're just going to sit and talk a bit. I'm here in the same room—just there behind the sheets, okay?"

I stood between the sheets; I could still feel her. I imagined her bent over Ilya, her hand in the child's hair. Her skin in the light of the TV—gray, white, pink. Her lips on Ilya's forehead. It was years since I'd touched another body. Years since I'd felt anything. And yet, what did it mean to Dori? What could it mean?

We went back to the others. Dori seemed calmer, soberer. She looked at me before we stepped out of the sheets. A glance, a smile, a hand on my shoulder. There was something there. Something between us.

11

While we'd been gone, Baby and the girls had decided to decamp into the private apartment. Baby had promised music—an entire record collection—and clothes for Lou and Cleo, who were still wearing the hotel bathrobes. I was uncomfortable with the suggestion and noticed that Dori, too, seemed unsure if it was a good idea to leave Ilya alone in the dining room under the present circumstances.

"We'll never be this young again!" Baby heaved herself up from the table, the bottle of tequila tucked under her arm. Lou and Cleo sensed our equivocation and offered to stay in the main building and start to get ready for the night. In the end it was Dori who turned the situation around and urged us to stay up.

"Ilya's gone back to sleep and we'll only be next door."

We put on our masks and slipped out, one by one, into the garden. The heat stood before us like a wall. We held hands. I went first, followed by Dori, Cleo, Lou,

Baby. Embers fell from the smoke like rain and settled on the gravel—specks of light glowing on the ground. The hotel wall was warm behind my back. I thought of the damage to the building. The cost of having the façade cleaned. The windows. I'd seen pictures of fire-damaged buildings without a pane of glass left. I made mental lists of things I had to repair before winter and things that could wait till the spring. I thought about ways of protecting the hotel better in the future. Even if the fire didn't cross the river, it was clear that my property wouldn't withstand such conditions forever. In the smoke at the far end of the field, about where the forest must begin, isolated streaks of flame stabbed the sky in quick succession. Flickered up and vanished. Here, then there, then here again. Closer than before. In the glow of the smoke, the maple stood black and alone.

It was hot in the apartment, and the sounds from outside were louder than in the dining room. The walls were thinner; the flat roof barely kept out the heat. We could hear the aid workers' shouts carried on the wind.

My room wasn't designed for guests. There was no table and nowhere to sit except the bed. Baby immediately took charge. She got Lou to set up a small record player and went into the next room with Cleo to fetch stools and plastic chairs and a folding table. Meanwhile I took Dori a bottle of water. I was worried about her;

she seemed drunker than the rest of us—more tired too. I guessed that her meds were to blame; it probably hadn't been smart to mix them with alcohol. She slurred her words and started sentences that changed tack halfway through or tailed off into laughter or random observations. Lou and Cleo followed Baby's instructions; they seemed to have accepted her as their host. It was fine with me. Baby belonged here; she'd known the hotel longer than I had. She found clothes for the girls—all old things of my aunt's, which surely wasn't a coincidence. Only the records were my mother's. Madonna, Stevie Nicks, Dolly Parton, Blondie.

Baby sat with her bottle and a fan on a folding chair that barely held her bulk. Cleo and Lou moved around the room in the old-fashioned light of the ceiling lamp, bodies close, foreheads touching. Dori and I were on my bed. I sat with my back against the wall, her head on my lap. My hand on her arm, in her hair.

Patti Smith, Bonnie Tyler.

The girls and Baby at the table. Baby telling them how she trained her pelvic floor while going about her daily life, tensing and relaxing it whenever she got the chance. Her hands at her belly, clenching and opening to illustrate what she was saying. "I squeeze everything in, then hold it—hold it—and release as I breathe out."

Baby urging the girls to do the same, assuring them they'd thank her for it—their lovers, future generations would thank her for it.

Dori singing softly, lagging behind the music. Dori laughing with her eyes shut.

Baby explaining why everyone called her Baby, though her real name was Mariette. A contract for diaper commercials, signed for her by her father when she was a year old. "Billboards and print ads—they don't offer that to everyone."

Dori forgetting her cigarette. Ash on my sheets, on her skin. I felt her body grow soft and heavy. I took the cigarette from her fingers, finished smoking it, lifted her head from my lap. Her damp, warm hair between my fingers. I lay down next to her. I could feel her back against my chest, the rise and fall of her breathing under my hand. Someone switched off the light. Whispers—the door—smoke—noises—smoke—silence. Dori and I, and out there the fire.

I was woken by someone gently shaking my shoulder. In the semidarkness I saw Baby bending over me. "Let her sleep."

I got up, everything sticking to me. I was dazed and thirsty; my head hurt, my throat was sore. Dori was also drenched in sweat, but she lay still, breathing deeply and steadily. I followed Baby into the bathroom. There, in the dim light, she told me. "The girl's gone."

I thought she was talking about one of the activists, Lou or Cleo, and turned with a shrug to head back to Dori. "Maybe she couldn't sleep," I said. "She'll be somewhere around."

It was Baby's face drained of irony that set my alarm bells ringing. She shook her head firmly and seriously, like after the death of my mother, my aunt, my grandfather. "Iris, we've looked everywhere. She isn't in the hotel."

It dawned on me that she was talking about Ilya. I wanted to wake Dori, but Baby held me back. "What can she do? Let her sleep. With any luck we'll bring the child back before she's noticed."

"She can't stay here alone," I said. "It isn't safe." But Baby took me by the arm. It wasn't safe anywhere.

She gave me a mask, led me outside and across the garden, pushed me along the wall through the hot smoke into the dining room, and closed the door. All the lights were on. The sheets had been taken down and lay in soft white folds on the stone floor, rolling hills and valleys. The mattresses in front of the TV were empty.

"The terrace door was open when we got back," Baby said at my side.

"How long has she been gone?" I'd lost all sense of time, didn't know how long I'd slept. Ilya by the river, Ilya on the burning field, Ilya alone, lost in the smoke. "She'll die out there."

I ran through the lobby into the kitchen, followed by Baby.

"Why didn't you fetch me sooner?" I pushed her hand from my arm.

"The girls are outside. Everyone's been informed. I've mobilized the volunteers. There are people everywhere, Iris. Everyone's looking for her, the whole town. We'll find her."

I thought of Dori's low voice telling Ilya we were in the same room. Imagined Ilya waking up and looking for us, her little form vanishing between the sheets.

12

Smoke. There was smoke everywhere. The fire had crossed the river. The garden fence hung in soft spools between the posts. I looked out over the dry grass of the field. People in masks were beating the fire with branches; flames seemed to spring up out of the ground. Islands of light, white in the red night. Black figures. Shouts everywhere. *Ilya, Ilya.*

Baby had stayed in the hotel by the phone. She was in charge of the search, knew who was where, kept tabs. I wandered over the field in my flip-flops, picking my way between dead birds, dead cats, clusters of embers. I half expected to find Ilya's body among them—a pale, fetal form barely bigger than the animals. Behind me was the town, the hotel, Dori in my bed. I prayed she'd stay asleep, prayed we'd bring Ilya back to her unscathed. Snatches of police announcements carried across the air, calling for evacuation, asking residents to assemble at the designated muster stations. The same announcements, over and over. The field was full of people; I recognized the familiar Bad Heim faces through the smoke. The greengrocer, the pharmacist, Paula's mother. Their skin gray, their masks gray, their eyes red and swollen behind protective goggles. Everyone had heard, but no one was carrying Ilya in their arms. No one had seen her.

Then the parcel postman found a leather slipper near the fence, and we knew she had to be out here somewhere, with only one slipper on, in her pajamas, crying, alone. Looking for her mother. How far could she have gotten, without a mask, without water?

With no hope of finding her, I made my way toward the river. I didn't recognize a thing, couldn't see half a yard in front of me, but I was convinced she had to be there, looking for Dori by the warm water—if there was any water left. I imagined her, Ilya with a stick, Ilya with a sun on her pajama top, as if the forest—our forest, this side of the forest—was still untouched by the fire. My skin and throat were raw from the heat, the smoke. There seemed to be nothing but heat and smoke.

Then a group of people—I don't know who—pushed me back. I can't remember much; all I know is that I tried to wriggle free and there were these arms I couldn't fight off. I shouted and cried under my mask, everything gummed up and dry, and those arms dragged rather than carried me all the way back to my garden, through a world that was changed beyond recognition. And all the time I was sure Ilya was in the forest. She was the fox I'd beaten to death, the dead birds, the dead fish, the dead cats.

Until I saw her. Asleep on Baby's chest. Her little face, her limp hair. Baby's hands holding her little body. Baby's chin, Baby's arms. Her low crooning, the little gold cross hanging on a chain next to the pale little face. And tucked in with Ilya, somewhere in the folds of skin and clothes—the gray cat.

Everyone still in town ended up in the hotel that night. I couldn't say how many. I gradually brought out what remained of my stores, and people hugged me and touched my back and pushed me onto chairs. In the middle of it all, Baby sat with the child in her arms—a huge Madonna, all flesh and silence.

The fire raged on. Those who left the hotel headed straight for the muster stations, Lou and Cleo among them. They were dressed in my aunt's clothes and carried their own things in plastic bags—clean, dry, folded. They hugged me goodbye. Lou's parents were on their way and would collect the girls from one of the emergency shelters.

"We'll be back." Their work wasn't over yet.

Baby had found Ilya—and the little cat—next door in her secret garden, in the shed where she'd provided shelter for the cats all through the long summer. Baby had found Ilya and brought her back.

In the early hours of the morning, the whole town breathed a sigh of relief. A meteorologist on TV announced that the heat had broken. Said the words *clouds* and *rain*. We waited. Peered through the windows, trying to tell smoke from cloud. Then it started to thunder. It was in this atmosphere of collective triumph that I saw Dori walk across the garden and come in at the terrace door. She'd slept through everything and had no idea what had happened. Her hair clung to her cheeks in wet strands; she looked pale and unhealthy, her eyes red, her lips cracked and dry. It was almost six. She saw Ilya, took her from Baby's arms, and asked shrilly over the noise what was going on, who all these people were, why she'd woken alone, in my bed. Baby got her a chair and a glass of water. Ilya was awake and safe. She'd eaten and drunk; Baby hadn't let her out of her sight for an instant.

I watched the scene from a distance.

I knew immediately. I could see it in the way Dori hugged Ilya, the way her gaze hung in the air without seeing. She'd been given a version of the story. She sat with the child in her arms, reproaching herself for her inadequacy. I saw how harshly she judged herself and

knew that her husband's accusations were surfacing
again, taking hold. *Selfish, destructive. Incapable of taking
care of Ilya.*

I wanted to tell her he was wrong. *The two of you are
better off without him. I'm here for you—for Ilya.* But what
right did I have to speak like that? What did I know
about Dori, about raising a child? I had nothing to offer
except a place that was barely inhabitable. No capital, no
prospects.

While outside the rain set in, falling in warm
threads through the smoke and making dusty rivulets
in the gravel—and while inside people stood at the windows crying with relief—Dori and Ilya sat at a distance.
I watched from reception. Dori's body had tensed up
again, her arms, the line of her jaw. I could tell she'd
panicked.

I was frightened by the chasm that gaped inside me.
That brief glimpse of a shared life was gone; I was alone
again. I told myself I'd lost nothing tangible. The house
by the lake, the family idyll—none of it had ever been
more than a fantasy. When Dori and Ilya left, nothing
would change for me; all I'd lose was a castle in the air.
I'd have my life back, I'd have peace and quiet again. I
could read, listen to music, do up the hotel.

I hid my thoughts and smiled at Baby, who had
come to stand next to me. She gave me sparkling wine,
clinked glasses with me, and drank. "Let me tell you
something, Iris," she said, following my gaze. "Life's a

buffet. Everyone's free to pick and choose." She squeezed my hand so tight it hurt. "Dori has to do what she thinks best for her and the kid. Don't yearn for her. You can't compete with that."

I knew that wasn't true. Anything would be better for Dori and Ilya than to go back. I felt a sudden horror at the thought of my lonely routine—couldn't understand how I'd managed to live like that for so long without noticing. There seemed to be nothing to look forward to. I would spend the rest of my life surrounded by empty chairs, staring out at the rain until the fires returned.

"Paula will be here soon," I said. "She's coming for her mother." But Baby already knew. I didn't tell her that Paula had also offered to take me in. Chances were, she knew that too.

"Everyone's free to pick and choose, Iris," she repeated. "Everyone has to look out for themselves."

13

Alexander Vargas arrived at the hotel toward evening. The locals had left by then, and Baby had headed home. I'd tidied the dining room and aired the bedrooms. The blue bag full of dead birds and fish was at the top of the garbage can. The air that had been trapped inside all summer could get out at last. It was over. The garden, the maple, the field, the forest—everything looked discolored and misshapen in the rain, and yet I had the feeling that given a little time and water and space, it wouldn't take much to restore things almost to their former glory.

Dori and Ilya were in their room; I was at reception. As soon as I saw the Mercedes pull up on the parking lot, I knew who was in it and why.

The engine was cut, the door opened, and a black umbrella appeared. Then a back in a white shirt. A hand, a flick of the wrist, the locks activated at the touch of a button.

We stood facing one another.

"Ms. Lehmann." White teeth, every hair in place. The voice I knew from the phone. "Thank you so much for helping my wife and me through this crisis." A firm handshake, a narrow gold ring.

Everything about him was suave, cordial, tasteful. He couldn't have been more agreeable. There was no reproach in his eyes; instead, he asked earnest questions about the state of the hotel, the situation in town.

"I can't imagine what this rain must mean to you."

Discreet jokes scattered here and there to dilute the gravity of the occasion. I could only guess what effect this man would have in a white doctor's coat.

I called Dori on the hotel phone. "Your husband's here." She thanked me as if there had never been any mention of him between us. Before I hung up I heard her say, "Ilya, Daddy's here."

Together, Vargas and I watched them walk along the veranda. Two gray figures in the twilight. Tack, tack, tack—Dori's strappy heels on the wet wood. Tap, tap, tap—Ilya's sandals. Then the reunion: the man with eyes only for the child, bending down to her, picking her up, smoothing a strand of wet hair from her face; Ilya only looking at him, letting him hold her—then glancing at Dori, who was standing next to her. Dori had tidied herself up, done her hair, put on makeup. Her hands were folded in front of her; she was wearing the gold bracelet and a wedding ring that I hadn't seen on her before. She smiled at her daughter, her gaze smooth, as if to say *At last we're together again.*

Vargas put the child down. "Has she eaten?" I looked from him to Dori. His perfectly styled hair, her perfectly styled hair. His white shirt, her light-colored dress. His ring, her ring.

After supper the three of them said good night and went back to their room. I cleared the table. It had stopped raining, but the sky was still overcast, and the air was filled with the sound of water running over the hard-baked ground. I walked across the garden, climbed over the black spools that had once been my fence, and stepped onto the field. It was hard to imagine that this wet land had been in flames just a few hours before; only the smell of wet carbon and the blackness of the ground and the trees remained as evidence. I felt chilly and realized I'd almost forgotten the feeling of unbearable heat on my skin. From the field I could see the window of number five in the sooty façade. The heat had warped the shutters, which closed with a slight gap, leaving a gaping black wedge in the middle. It must be dark in the room. I wondered what was going on in there. Were they lying on the big bed together, with Ilya between them? Or was one of them in the armchair? Were there whispered conversations, reproaches, apologies?

I walked slowly back toward the hotel and garden. That afternoon, locals with umbrellas had gone around the field, gathering up the wet bodies of the animals that had died. Anything burned was disposed of.

The hard-baked soil wasn't ready for all this water. I had to dig a channel at the end of the garden, pile up sandbags. I hoped the groundwater would rise in the winter, although the earth was so dry. I hoped the land wouldn't be washed away, hoped the river wouldn't burst its banks.

I stopped at the fence, about four or five feet from Dori's door. All was still. I looked out into the black night. The smoldering fire's edge, which had streaked the dark forest all summer, was gone. I tried to tell myself that it was no longer any concern of mine what happened to Dori and Ilya, but I felt a growing sense of unease.

Nearby something moved. I saw a glimmer of red and then Baby's face behind it. She offered me a cigarette. "Nothing to stop us now." Baby's brown eyes on my face, just behind the flame.

"I saw the car," she said. We smoked. "Would you rather be alone?"

I shook my head. I was glad to have Baby there. Baby, who belonged to the hotel and Bad Heim. Who'd known Grandad and Auntie, my mother, my grand-mother. She heaved herself, puffing and blowing, over what was left of the fence, gripped my shoulders, and pulled me into her warm body, her armpits, the smell of her. Soap, sweat, tobacco, washing powder. I remembered the soft shape of her body. I remembered sleeping next to her in front of the TV after Mom died, her face close to mine as she chewed and belched and licked her greasy fingers. I remembered her hand stroking my back. *There, there, go to sleep.* I remembered her guttural laugh.

She held me tight while we smoked. Then she let me go. She stubbed out our cigarettes on the wet fence post and put them in her fanny pack.

"Did you know that your auntie and I used to sit in the next room when your grandad was giving your mom one of his talking-tos?"

I nodded. Baby had told me the stories. How they'd sat and listened at the wall, waiting for Grandad to leave my mother be.

We headed for number four. I'd cleaned it that afternoon, given it an airing, stripped the beds. It smelled the way I liked it—a vinegary, lemony scent no longer drowned out by the endless reek of smoke. Baby pushed the armchair to the wall. We could hear Vargas's voice coming quietly from the next room. I couldn't make out what he was saying, but the spate of words was enough. On and on he went; there seemed no end to it. I didn't hear a peep from Dori. I imagined her standing there like a child, nodding and nodding and nodding. Taking everything as it came.

I felt Baby's hand on my arm. She shook her head. There was nothing we could do.

I thought of Baby and Auntie at the wall while Mom sat on the chair in the next room, forbidden to move. While Grandad talked and talked. While it turned midnight, one o'clock, two o'clock, and no one could sleep till he'd finished. My mother, because she wasn't allowed. Because she'd broken some rule, done something she shouldn't have done, and couldn't figure out what. Auntie, because she didn't want to leave her sister alone with Grandad. Baby, because she wanted to be ready to intervene at the first blow, jump up and burst through the door, pull my mother from the chair and carry her off. As a child I'd always imagined that it was Grandad she'd protected: she'd made sure he didn't do anything bad.

In the light of the bedside lamp I saw Baby's face at the wall, her big shadow, her heaving chest, which rubbed against the wallpaper with every breath. I saw her soft hands, the tendons under her skin. What would have become of Mom without Baby? What would have become of Auntie, of Grandad, of me?

I leaned back in the armchair, knowing I could sleep because she was there. I thought of Dori and Ilya next door in the dark, and scenes from the previous night came back to me: the heat, the fire, Dori and me on my bed, Dori and me between the sheets, the search for Ilya. I thought of the little unit we'd formed: Lou and Cleo, Baby and Dori and me. It was as if we'd been thrown together by the events surrounding us, compressed into a single point in time. Now it was over. We were individuals again, blown apart as soon as the pressure was off.

Outside it was raining and next door, perhaps, Ilya's hand lay on the little sun that rose and fell, rose and fell under a surge of words—and this time it wasn't a voice message that could be cut off at will. *Narcissist, egoist. Mentally unfit. Not right in the head. No kind of mother for the child.*

At dawn it finally went quiet in number five. Baby stretched her arms over her head, yawned at me, and heaved herself out of the armchair. She hadn't had to jump into action.

We drank a cup of coffee, looking quietly out at our field and at the maple in front that stood out like a black tooth. We parted at the fence post. Baby clapped me on the shoulder.

"I'll look in again this evening," she said as she walked away. "With some goulash."

I showered and dressed. It had started to rain again. I walked into town along sidewalks awash with water and bought rolls, butter, jam, milk, apples, peaches, meat, potatoes, rice. No face mask, the air cool on my skin. The foil had gone from the windows; mysterious shapes in black, gold, and silver bulged out of wet garbage cans. Burned things, emergency blankets, masks.

Back in the hotel I fixed breakfast for the family. I laid the table: three plates, three cups, two knives. I cut fruit, made coffee, put rolls in a basket, butter on a dish. Honey, jam, napkins. A little jug of milk.

Later I watched them from reception. Father, mother, child. Alexander, Dori, Ilya. They were speaking quietly, he in long sentences, she in short ones. Dori nodded a lot and kept her eyes on her plate. They drank coffee and milk, they ate fruit. The cool sun fell through the freshly cleaned windows onto the table, bathing everything in white. Dori was wearing the same dress with a cardigan over the top, the same strappy shoes. Her smile, her movements—everything about her seemed smaller. She sat there, reduced to pure function.

Shining hair. Clean clothes. Clean fingernails. The fruit bowl passed from hand to hand, wedding rings in the sunlight. Dori's bracelet.

A family. A childhood.

I thought of something Dori had said when we were sitting around the table with Lou and Cleo and Baby. "I'm the only family she has now." And I thought to myself that it had been enough. That what Ilya needed was a mother who had the space to be more than just a mother. The space to be a whole person. In all my thoughts of my mother that was something I hadn't grasped until now. She had never let them keep her down.

I saw Dori only once more before they left. She smiled without looking at me and put the key on the counter. I wanted to ask, *Are you sure you're doing the right thing?* I wanted to say, *You know you can stay, you know you can always come back.* But the person I might have pleaded with was no longer there. "I need your IDs," I said instead.

She nodded. This time she found them right away. There was her name on a little plastic card and Ilya's name in a child's passport. *Dorota Vargas. Ilya Elisabeth Vargas.* I didn't comment, but entered the address into the bookings system and returned the documents. After a moment's hesitation I asked for her phone number. Later, when they'd left, I saw on the internet that Ansel, the name she'd given when she arrived, was her maiden name. Dorota Ansel was the name she'd acted under.

Vargas crossed the lobby, nodded, then glanced at the clock hanging at reception. He'd already paid the bill, rounding up generously. He carried Ilya and the small suitcase out to the car. She and I waved to each other. I would have liked to give her a hug and had got out the suitcase house ready as a gift for her, but her father seemed eager to get going, and I left it. She didn't need it; she was sure to have plenty of toys at home.

"I really hope all goes well for you," I said quietly to Dori.

She stared at me, her face smooth, her little tooth hidden behind her painted smile. Then she shrugged as if there were only one option open to her anyway—only one life.

But as she was walking away—as the car door and then the trunk slammed shut outside—she said, "I have a lot to make amends for now."

As if my part in it had made things even worse for her. I said nothing.

She raised a hand before stepping out the door. "Thank you for all you did."

I stared out the window, watching her go. She got into the passenger seat and her face vanished behind the gray sky reflected on the windshield.

14

When I cleaned Dori and Ilya's room I found two things: the book of poems and the bracelet that Dori had lost in my car. It occurred to me that we'd never talked about where she'd been that night. Presumably it had been an aimless drive—her way of dealing with insomnia. I felt a flicker of hope at the thought that her future journeys might have a destination—that it was only a six-hour drive from Berlin to Bad Heim.

I picked up the book and lay down on the unmade bed. The window and door were open, and wind blew in from the field, through the rain.

On the first page I found the poem that Dori had once quoted:

he eats me up till nothing's left
he eats me up till nothing's left
he eats me up till nothing's left
he eats me up until

The dangling line at the end of the poem had been underscored in thin, gray pencil.

An opening, a promise. *He eats me up until*—didn't that mean it had to end at some point?

I lay and read. As I turned the pages, the old Bad Heim unfolded before me, but also stories and memories. Tents made of sheets, two children in a magic forest, a little talking dog. With every word, with every line, I saw her more clearly. Ada Lumin. The blond hair, the familiar face, the look of someone holding a rifle.

Air filled the room. Through the door I saw the little gray cat slinking through the garden. There was a smell of rain. At last, rain. I felt myself grow cold.

I thought of the summer when Grandfather had dug the pond and had the veranda built. Mom on the phone, Mom at the window, in bed, on the lounger. Mom writing. I'd always thought she was keeping a diary.

I thought of Grandad carrying our bags, Grandad in his undershirt in the dust. My mother at a distance. Impassive. Hard on him. Our unpacked suitcase against the wall behind the door. It was always the same, I thought. Always the same decision—to go or stay.

I thought of Dori. I thought of my mother and of Paula.
Of the starlings in the sky.
Circling, circling.

Someone called my name.
It was Baby, with the goulash.

ABOUT THE AUTHOR

Franziska Gänsler was born in Augsburg, Germany, in 1987. She studied art and English in Berlin, Vienna, and Augsburg. In 2020 she was short-listed for the Blogbuster Prize and was a finalist at Berlin's 28th Open Mike competition. Gänsler lives in Augsburg and Berlin. *Eternal Summer* is her debut novel.

ABOUT THE TRANSLATOR

Imogen Taylor was born in London in 1978 and has lived in Berlin since 2001. She is the translator of Sascha Arango, Dirk Kurbjuweit, and Melanie Raabe, among others. Her translation of Sasha Marianna Salzmann's *Beside Myself* (Other Press, 2020) was short-listed for the 2021 Helen & Kurt Wolff Translator's Prize and the 2020 Schlegel-Tieck Prize.